Every journey starts with a single step

ANNIE: The dandelion. Strong and determined, this widow has recently been promoted to vice president of her bank, so her life should be on the upswing, right? If only she could break the news to her former mother-in-law that she'd found a new man in her life....

VIOLET: The rose. Delicate and conservative, this retired teacher shares a wonderful relationship with her daughter-in-law, so why can't things just stay the same? But if her strong convictions frown upon Annie's new direction, what do they say about the new addition to the family...?

SUMMER: The bad tomato. Dumped on the doorstep of her do-good aunt, just how did a blond, cherubic eight-year-old transform into a Goth teen with a crush on black eyeliner? Annie's niece is three miles of bad road, but then again, she's never had the support of a loving and committed family until now....

Will these three women be able to bridge the generational gap and find the way home together?

Diane Amos

lives with her husband, Dave, in a small town north of Portland, Maine. They have four grown children, a finicky Siamese named Sabrina and an energetic miniature dachshund named Molly. Diane is an established Maine artist. Her paintings are in private collections across the United States. She is a Golden Heart finalist and winner of the Maggie Award for Excellence. For more information about Diane and her books, check out her Web site at www.dianeamos.com.

THE Next™ NOVEL

Diane Amos

A LONG

WALK

HOME

A LONG WALK HOME

copyright © 2005 Diane Amos

i s b n 0 3 7 3 2 3 0 5 0 8

This edition published by arrangement with Harlequin Books S.A.

® and TM are trademarks of the publisher. Trademarks indicated with
® are registered in the United States Patent and Trademark Office, the
Canadian Trade Marks Office and in other countries.

TheNextNovel.com

 HARLEQUIN®

PRINTED IN U.S.A.

Acknowledgments

Michelle Libby
Talented author and president of
the Maine chapter of RWA

Special thanks to:
Portland Police Officer Chuck Libby
for sharing information about
police procedure.
Any mistakes that I've made or liberties
that I've taken are completely my own.

Joyce Lamb
A talented author
critique partner
and
good friend

CHAPTER 1

"What, no chocolate cake!" the three of us said in unison to the waiter who'd announced the unthinkable before handing us dessert menus and retreating to the kitchen.

Mallory turned to Carrie and me. "Life's a bitch."

Carrie nodded. "Which is why I'm glad to have you two as my good friends."

I had to agree. My friends kept me grounded, and life…well, had been filled with the unexpected. I'd learned long ago that nothing was as it seemed. And I never took anything for granted.

I drank a sip of my martini, lifted my glass to theirs and said with much dignity, "Life's a bi-otch."

Carrie giggled. "Since when are you so polite?"

I took another small swallow. I rarely drank, and when I did, I got dizzy on the fumes. "As the new vice president of the loan department at Portland National Bank, I must conduct myself with decorum."

Mallory raised her glass and announced, "In honor of Ms. Annie Jacobs, our hoity-toity pal and Madame

Vice President, 'life is a bitch' will forever be banned from our vocabulary and from now on be referred to as LIB."

Carrie's forehead wrinkled. "Huh, shouldn't that be LIAB?"

"I took a little artistic license and dropped the A. Besides, LIB sounds better."

For a moment Carrie pondered what Mallory had said. "You're right."

"I'll drink to that," I said as I polished off my martini, which had started out tasting like paint thinner—not that I knew that for a fact—and had improved with each swallow.

Our waiter, John, returned. He was tall, with a wiry build and dark hair. Thick eyelashes framed his sapphire-blue eyes.

Mallory smiled at the hunky guy who looked young enough to be her son—if she'd had a son. Neither of us had children, which suited us fine.

Children complicated matters.

They were messy.

And selfish.

Although I was happy with my life, something inside me stirred.

Disappointment?

Ridiculous.

I was thirty-seven—tick-tock—time had run out.

I'd gotten over the need to cradle a child in my

arms. Plus, my chances of becoming a mother had died eighteen months ago along with Paul, my husband, the love of my life.

The man whom I'd thought could do no wrong.

But he'd betrayed me.

Mallory pointed a manicured finger at our waiter. "Since you don't have double fudge chocolate cake, then I'll have raspberry swirled chocolate cheesecake."

He directed a killer grin at my friend.

I wasn't surprised. At thirty-nine, Mallory Bourque was the total package, a blond male magnet with hazel eyes, big breasts, long legs and a great personality. If Mallory were a flower she'd be a gardenia, not because she was fragile, but because men wanted to tend to her needs. Mallory owned the Ooh La La, a specialty lingerie shop in the Old Port area of Portland, Maine.

"What about your friends?" he asked, unable to tear his gaze from Mallory.

By his dazed expression, I knew he was a goner. He wasn't the first and wouldn't be the last. By the time we got our tab, Mallory would have his phone number and the promise of a hot date. She preferred younger men, no strings attached. Just fun and games.

"I'll have the chocolate cheesecake." I could tell my words hadn't penetrated.

Neither had Carrie's, "Me, too."

Talk about being invisible.

Mallory bowed her lower lip into a perfect pout.

"They'll have the same and bring us another round of drinks."

He blinked a couple times, I suspected, to clear his head.

"Sure, be right back." Then he forced himself to look away from the goddess who'd captured his heart—and if not his heart then surely his lust.

Carrie straightened her napkin over her knees and turned toward Mallory. "I'd have a meltdown if a man looked at me like that."

"He is a cutie," Mallory replied. "I wouldn't mind having him for dessert."

Carrie Hudson was thirty-five, five-three, always on a diet and a single mother of seven-year-old twin boys. Her blue eyes sparkled, and she blushed easily. She reminded me of a pink carnation. Resilient and pretty.

After my husband died, I'd eventually discovered I was like a dandelion. Not the prettiest flower, but strong, determined and, when push came to shove, I didn't take no for an answer. There were worse things in life than being compared to a weed that persisted against all odds.

Every Friday evening after work, the three of us met at DiMillo's, a car ferry converted into a floating restaurant known for its good food and ambiance on the Portland waterfront. Soon it would be too cold to be outside so we'd decided to sit on the top deck, enjoy the unseasonably warm September weather and watch the boats going by.

We always ordered a decadent dessert and drinks, which for me was usually a diet Pepsi, but tonight was special. I'd gotten the promotion I'd worked so hard for, and no one orders a Pepsi on such an occasion. So I'd decided to live dangerously and drink a martini. I wasn't crazy about the taste, but I loved olives so I couldn't lose.

Below us in the marina, cruisers and sailboats in their slips swayed as gentle waves washed ashore. The smell of salt, seaweed and fish permeated the air. In the distance seagulls cawed and a bell buoy clanged.

A light breeze ruffled my hair as I leaned back and thought with satisfaction about my promotion. I'd worked hard and deserved this. But a person didn't always get what he/she deserved. I'd lucked out. My life was on a steep uphill path, and I'd equipped myself for the climb. Even my relationship with Tony was about to take a major turn. We loved each other. I was happy. Only now, I'd have to tell my mother-in-law, Violet, about him.

"Hey, why the long face?" Mallory asked.

"I was thinking about how everything is clicking into place, except…" I sucked in my lower lip, a bad habit I'd tried unsuccessfully to stop. "I'm meeting Violet tomorrow to break the news that Tony is moving in."

"You're an adult, and you don't owe your mother-in-law an explanation," Mallory pointed out.

"Yes I do. She's been like a mother to me since my mom moved away. She's the only family I've got. And I don't want to hurt her, but I can't put off telling her about Tony any longer. She'll never approve of my seeing another man. And to her, we'll be living in sin."

Mallory rolled her eyes. "No one thinks like that anymore."

"You haven't met Violet. She's a staunch Catholic and very old-fashioned."

Carrie looked thoughtful. "Too bad you didn't tell her about Tony months ago."

"I tried, but each time I'd start to tell her, she'd interrupt and say something about Paul. She worships her son's memory, and to hear her talk you'd think he died yesterday. She isn't ready to hear I'm with another man."

Mallory straightened. "Tell her what a jerk her precious son was."

"I couldn't do that to her."

Carrie ran a finger over the condensation on the side of her glass. "This might be the wakeup call she needs to accept Paul's death and go on with her life."

"Maybe," I said, doubting that would happen.

Violet would never give her blessing to Tony and me living together. Not that I needed her approval, but even before Paul's death we'd formed a strong bond and a friendship that until now, I'd thought indestructible.

* * *

"My, don't you look pretty this morning," Vi said as she opened the kitchen and caught me in a tight hug; her mouth brushed my cheek.

I felt warm, safe and at home.

Surely she'd understand. If only I'd told her sooner. She had a right to know that her son's widow had fallen in love with another man.

Panic swelled inside and threatened to cut off my breathing.

Vi reminded me of a rose, delicate and beautiful.

"You smell good," I said amazed at how steady my voice sounded when she pulled away, took my hand and led me into the kitchen.

"My Avon lady gave me a few samples that I'm trying out. This one's called Lilacs in Bloom. I'm thinking of ordering some. Nice, don't you think?"

"Yes." I put the box I'd been carrying on the table and untied the string. "I picked up a raspberry strudel at the bakery on my way over here."

She filled the kettle with water and set it on the burner. While putting cups, spoons and napkins on the table, she smiled at me. "You're always so thoughtful, and it means so much to me. I couldn't wait for you to arrive. I have a special gift for you in honor of your new job," she said, her gray eyes glowing with excitement.

Many women complained about their mothers-in-law, but I'd been blessed. Vi had been my rock, my strength, my family for years. Shortly before Paul's death, my mother had remarried and moved to Texas with her husband. It wasn't that she didn't care about me, but she was immersed in her new life. We spoke on the phone several times a month and visited a couple times a year.

No one knew for sure where my sister Dana and her thirteen-year-old daughter Summer lived, but according to the postcard from California I'd received months ago, they were fine. Could I wire her some cash and please hurry because she was moving again? As soon as she'd found a job, she'd repay me, which I knew would never happen. Against my mother's advice, I'd sent the money and an extra couple hundred dollars hoping against very slim odds that my sister would use some of it on my niece.

Vi looked so happy, so unaware of what I was going to say. Guilt gnawed at my insides. She waved for me to follow her into her bedroom. She was nearing sixty, and when she smiled, which was rare, she looked much younger. Usually her mouth turned down, her brow furrowed and her eyes filled with grief.

I hated to cause her more pain. She'd already suffered too much.

As she crossed the room and opened a cedar chest, I noticed the pictures of Paul on her dresser. There was a cute one of him as a toddler playing in the sand, another on his graduation from college and several of us on our wedding day. Our smiles wide and our hearts full. When we'd believed love conquered all.

Vi reached way in the back of the chest and pulled out a small package. She turned, took my hand, and nestled a velvet box into my palm. "I'm sure you already know this, but I want to say again how much I love you. You've been like a daughter to me." Her eyes misted. Blinking away tears, she reached into her apron pocket and blew her nose on a tissue. After sucking in a long breath, she continued, "I'd promised myself I wouldn't get all mushy and sentimental, but you know how I am. If you and Paul had had babies, I'd planned to give you this in the hospital to enjoy for a while, then pass on to the next generation."

As I cupped the box in my hand, a faint scent of cedar rose to my nostrils.

"Go ahead, open it," Vi, said, looking happy. "I can't wait to see your face."

Positioning a finger on either side of the box, I lifted the lid and looked down at a beautiful emerald ring that I'd seen only once before on Vi's finger on the day Paul and I said our vows. It had belonged to her mother. Vi had explained she'd kept it locked away in a safe-deposit box for fear of losing it.

"I can't accept this," I said, overwhelmed with emotion. Love and guilt consumed me. How could I tell her about Tony? How could I not?

"It's a gift from me to you. The decision has already

been made. You've worked hard to earn your promotion. I'm proud of you. My only regret is that I didn't give you this ring a lot sooner."

I was a traitor, about to send her world spinning out of control. I didn't know what to say. My legs felt like rubber, shaky and about to give way. Before I could muster a coherent thought, the kettle on the stove whistled, and Vi ran out to pour our tea.

As if in a dream I walked into the kitchen, still clutching the box, stealing another glance at the precious green stone twinkling in the light coming through the window. I watched Vi slide generous pieces of strudel onto two dishes, felt my throat constrict with dread, felt perspiration on my palms as I sat and caught my breath.

"So aren't you going to try it on," she said indicating the ring. "I had it sized to fit your finger, but the jeweler at Day's said if it needs to be adjusted to bring it back, and he'll do it right away."

I set the box down and met her expectant gaze.

Where to begin.

I wanted to explain how many times I'd come over here planning to tell her about Tony. I wanted to tell her how much she meant to me, but that would only postpone the inevitable. Fearing I might back down again and leave without telling her the truth, I knew I had to dive right into the subject. Or she might hear the news from someone else.

And that would be worse.

"I need to tell you something that might upset you."

Worry etched deep lines around her mouth and eyes. "Are you sick?"

"No, it's nothing like that."

"Thank the good Lord. I don't know what I'd do without you. What in heaven's name is wrong?"

I paused and tried to choose the right words. "Nothing is wrong. As a matter of fact it's good news. Sort of."

Confusion clouded her eyes. "Now I'm really puzzled."

"I've met someone. His name is Anthony Marino."

She collapsed into the chair and heaved a sigh. I waited for the aftershocks to subside.

"I'd like you to meet him," I said, my voice trembling. "You'll like him. I think Paul would have liked him, too."

"How long have you been seeing this Tony?"

I considered lying, but that would only compound the guilt of not having told her sooner. "Seven months."

Her features twisted in disbelief. "Surely, it's not serious, or you'd have told me about this man sooner."

I curled my hands around the warm mug of tea, tried to steady my grip, tried to soften the impact.

I went for broke, no more skirting the issue. "He loves me, and I love him."

"What about Paul?"

Paul's dead.

Too blunt, too hurtful. I sucked in my lower lip and blew out a soft breath. "I can't bring Paul back."

"You mourned your husband for less than a year," she said, her eyes filling with tears. "How can you do this?"

She made it sound as though I'd cheated on her son.

I wanted to ask her how long I should mourn a man who'd betrayed me. I considered shattering her distorted image of her son, but I couldn't do that to her.

"I was a good wife to Paul while he was alive. And I don't want to live the rest of my life alone."

Avoiding eye contact, she stared across the room. Tense silence stretched between us until I could hear my heartbeat pounding in my ears.

"I just need a chance to accept this," she said, her voice hollow. "I know Paul is gone. I know we can't bring him back. You're young. You have a right to be happy. Maybe you'll even have children. I could be their grandmother," she said, a tinge of hope creeping into her tone.

Tony already had three children from his first marriage. He'd made it clear he didn't want any more babies. I understood. Plus, I'd reached the point in my life where I no longer yearned to hold an infant in my arms and to watch my child grow: first steps, first words, being loved unconditionally.

At least I didn't think I did.

"I'm a bit old to have babies," I said, not wanting to lead her astray.

"You're still young. Nowadays I can't turn on the news without hearing of some actress having a baby in her forties. Lots of women are having children later in life. You could, too." She sighed again and looked at me. "I apologize for overreacting a few minutes ago. I just never thought of you with another man. I can't fathom seeing you with anyone but my Paul, but that's silly of me." She paused for a moment as if absorbing what she couldn't change. "Maybe we can discuss your Tony in a few days after I've had a chance to think this through." Her voice softened. "You and Paul were perfect together."

I'd thought so, too.

We were far from perfect, only I didn't discover that until after his funeral.

Vi reached across the table and took my hands in hers. "I don't blame you for trying to find that close bond again. Give me a little while to think about this. I'm sure in time I can accept that you've found another man to love you. I certainly can't blame you for wanting to get married again."

I'd dreaded this most, but I'd come this far, it wasn't time to back down. "Tony is moving in tomorrow, but we don't intend to get married."

Vi's face flushed, and she pulled her hands away. She made the sign of the cross and closed her eyes. When she opened them again, I saw disbelief and shame.

"This is a disgrace to Paul's memory."

CHAPTER 2

Two weeks later on my way home from work I stopped at the florist and arranged for a bouquet of red roses to be delivered to Violet. Since she was the most stubborn woman I'd ever met, I knew she wouldn't make the first move. I'd missed her. I signed the card, *Love, Annie.* Now it was up to her to respond.

I pulled my white Volvo into my driveway next to Tony's silver Porsche. I owned a modest three-bedroom cape in Gray, Maine, a small town on the outskirts of Portland. After Paul died, I'd used some of the money from his life insurance to redecorate and try to wash away some of the painful memories. I'd moved out of the master bedroom and chose the smaller room which faced my backyard and my flower garden. I'd added a sunroom off the deck and invested in a hot tub, something I'd wanted for years but Paul had considered frivolous.

I'd felt a deep sense of power the day the hot tub had arrived. Although I suspected my purchase might have been partially an act of defiance, it was also a milestone: the day I started to take charge of my life.

Tony owned a house in Saco that he planned to rent on a month to month tenancy. Neither of us was willing to surrender our independence.

As I opened the kitchen door, the spicy smell of oregano and thyme teased my nostrils. Tony stood at the stove, his broad shoulders hunched as he stirred the pasta sauce. He turned and smiled at me. Due to the steam, a stray lock of his deep brown hair curled over his forehead. He hated that his hair waved, but I loved running my fingers through the thick, silky strands.

"How's my Italian?" I asked, walking toward him for the kiss I craved. "I'm famished."

"I'm horny."

"What else is new," I said with a laugh.

"You're to blame, always giving me that 'she-devil' look."

I laughed. "What you see is the look of a starving woman."

"Starving, huh, in more ways than one, I bet."

"You're incorrigible."

"When it comes to you, I am," he said, wrapping his arms around me. His lips claimed mine in a kiss filled with need and passion.

Tony pulled away a little and leaned his forehead against mine. "That's some welcome. Say the word, and I'll abandon this meal."

"Not so fast, Bucko." I playfully wrenched free. "What's a woman gotta do around here to get fed?"

"She needs to stop seducing the cook," he said with that crooked grin I loved.

I undid the top two buttons on my blouse and exposed a little of my white slip. "You ain't seen nothin' yet."

"You're a wicked tease," he said, lifting his right eyebrow. "You'd better plan on tipping the help…if you know what I mean."

"Incorrigible…"

"That's because you're a wanton sexy hussy."

I glanced down at my gray pinstriped business suit. "I'd hate to think how you'd react if I were wearing a camisole and garters."

"That's an interesting premise. Go ahead, I dare you…." His smile deepened. His eyes darkened a few shades.

"I hate to disappoint you, but I was planning on changing into jeans and a flannel shirt."

"You'll look sexy no matter what you wear." He picked up the wooden spoon and winked.

"Hold that thought," I said as I turned and walked through the living room and into my bedroom.

In the short time we'd been living together, I'd come to enjoy the camaraderie. And the dynamite sex. More than lovers, we were friends. Tony made me happy.

We completed each other….

But I'd thought the same thing about Paul.

How could I trust my judgment?

* * *

The following Friday morning after a meeting, my administrative assistant Roberta greeted me. "Here's a list of the people who called while you were out. The Thompsons are hoping to close early next week."

"Please call them back and set up an appointment for Tuesday." I took the tablet she handed me and glanced down. One name stuck out. Violet Jacobs. My heartbeat quickened.

"Thanks," I said, hurrying into my office and shutting the door.

I braced myself as I punched in the number. Vi was a gracious woman. She wasn't the type of person who'd call to argue or reiterate that I was a disgrace to her son's memory. Though I was certain her opinion of my situation hadn't changed, I was hoping we could get beyond that.

"The Jacobs residence, Violet Jacobs speaking."

Violet had lived alone for years, since she'd ordered her cheating husband to leave, yet she'd insisted on answering the phone as though others resided in her house.

"Vi, it's Annie."

I heard her inhale a slow breath. "Annie, how nice to hear from you. The roses you sent are beautiful. How thoughtful of you."

"I wanted you to know that I still care," I said, swallowing back the knot in my throat.

"I've missed you, too. I was hoping you could come over for lunch tomorrow. Alone, just you and me…like old times."

Clear and to the point.

Tony wasn't welcome.

But I was willing to compromise. Plus, Tony had to work tomorrow. His architectural firm was preparing a bid on a new mall. "Yes, is noon good for you?"

"Perfect."

We spoke for a few more minutes about incidentals: the rising cost of gas, oil heat and the weather. Once we'd exhausted topics of no importance, we hung up.

I spun around in my desk chair and while glancing out at the Portland skyline, I realized how much I'd missed hearing from Vi. I hoped tomorrow we could start to bridge the gap in our relationship.

Later that day I met Mallory and Carrie at DiMillo's. The hostess led us to a table by a window. The light mist that had started falling that afternoon had become intermittent rain which now pelted the pane of glass. A raw, crisp wind stirred the ocean into choppy waves, causing boats in the harbor to sway on their moorings.

We sat down and took the menus from the hostess who filled our glasses with water. "Your server will be right with you."

"Anything new?" Carrie asked me.

"I'm meeting Vi for lunch tomorrow."

"That's great," Carrie replied.

"You keep up a strong front," Mallory said. "Don't let her make you feel guilty about wanting a life for yourself. There's nothing wrong with you and Tony living together. You're adults for cripes sake."

"This isn't about who's right and who's wrong. I want us to be friends."

"What if that's not possible?" Mallory asked.

I'd wondered the same thing. Would I have to choose between Tony and Vi? "Then I'll deal with that, too."

John, the waiter we'd had last week, walked past our table. He and Mallory exchanged searing glances as he hurried into the kitchen.

"Let me guess…" I covered my mouth with my right hand. "Something's going on between you two."

Carrie fanned her face. "Something hot, hot, hot!"

"And it's a wonder I can still walk," Mallory said with a low laugh.

Carrie shook her head. "I'd love to find a nice guy and settle down. But no one's willing to take on the responsibility of a ready-made family."

Mallory looked down at the dessert menu. "Men are afraid of getting married. But they're always willing to move in for a week of fun and games, right, Annie?"

I was a bit irritated that Mallory would compare what I had with Tony to her fly-by-night encounters.

"Why are you asking me? I know nothing about sampling the flavor of the week."

Mallory's mouth curved into a wide smile. "Neither of you know what you're missing." She set the menu down. "Most men are terrified of commitment. They do a convincing song and dance about love and how you don't need a piece of paper to prove how you feel. But it's the same bull."

What Mallory had said sounded very familiar, and it stung. True, I'd agreed with Tony: marriage was just a piece of paper, a certificate that bound two people together until the good times disappeared.

The concept of marriage was a farce.

It was far more sensible to live together and know that person was there because he/she wanted to be there, not because that piece of paper said they couldn't leave.

It made sense, so why did I feel as though I needed to defend my live-in relationship? Plus, I certainly wasn't ready for more than a bedmate—a sexy, turn my legs to mush, kissable bedmate.

Mallory turned to Carrie. "If you want a man, then pretend you aren't looking for 'the one.'"

"You mean lie?"

Mallory nodded. "I prefer to think of it as bending the truth a little."

"I'm a mother so I have to project a certain image."

"You need to loosen up," Mallory said, her gaze following John as he took an older couple's order several tables away. "Hmmm-hmmm, nice butt."

"Not bad," I said, tapping my fingernail against the water glass. "For a kid."

Mallory's hazel eyes sparkled. "John's in his second year of college at the University of Southern Maine."

"You're kidding," Carrie said, her cheeks flushing crimson.

Mallory uttered a deep laugh. "Before you call the cops on me, it's not as bad as it sounds. He was in the navy for a while and went back to school. He's thirty-one."

"I don't know if I could ever marry a younger man," Carrie said.

"I don't intend to marry him. Though I'd like him to stick around for a while. He's very talented in bed."

"That sounds awful, like you're using him," Carrie said, looking troubled.

Carrie was the more sensitive of my two friends. When it came to men, she was too nice, too willing to believe what they said. And she ended up hurt.

"We both know where we stand," Mallory replied. "No one's going to get hurt. And there's nothing wrong with enjoying each other's company. Especially when the guy is so yummy. Enough about me, how's Tony?"

"We're getting along really well. I was concerned I'd feel as though he was invading my space, but we have enough alone time that it isn't a problem," I replied.

Carrie took a sip of water. "I'm looking for someone

really special, a man who'll want to spend his spare time with me and the boys. Someone I can trust."

"I think that breed is extinct," Mallory said.

Carrie sighed. "I'm afraid you may be right."

"Have you started to notice Tony's little annoying habits yet?" Mallory asked.

"Nope, maybe he doesn't have any." I knew that would stir up Mallory.

"When you least expect it, you'll start noticing the cap off the toothpaste, the butter left out on the counter, in the morning dirty dishes in the sink that weren't there when you went to bed. That's when I usually give the guy the heave-ho. And since there are no strings attached, it'll be easy for you to move on, too."

Mallory didn't understand my relationship with Tony. We weren't planning to get married, but both of us considered our relationship permanent. "He enjoys cooking for me," I said. "And he brings me flowers every week. I see us growing old together."

Mallory threw me a bright smile. "That's always a possibility, but if it doesn't work out, there are no strings. It'll be a lot easier to move on to the next flavor of the month."

After soaking in the hot tub and sharing a couple glasses of wine, Tony and I made love twice: first on the lounge in the sunroom, the rain beating down on the glass-paneled ceiling, our joining frantic and exciting.

Overhead lightning arced across the black sky as thunder rumbled. Then Tony picked me up, walked into the house and laid me down on my bed. No rush this time, slow, thorough and breathtaking.

He'd fallen asleep shortly afterward, his arm wrapped around me, my head against his chest. I couldn't stop thinking how fortunate I was.

My life was nearly perfect.

I'd dozed off and was awakened around three by the phone. Two rings and the answering machine picked up. Since I'd never gotten around to having a jack installed in this room, I hurried into the living room.

"Annie, it's Mom."

I grabbed the receiver, dropped it on the floor and scrambled to pick it up. "What's wrong?"

I saw Tony coming toward me, clad only in a pair of dark boxers. He placed his hands over my shoulders, and I instantly felt stronger. Thank goodness he was here with me now.

"It's your sister," Mom said, between sobs. "They found her unconscious in a sleazy apartment complex in Los Angeles. She was rushed to the hospital. According to the doctor I spoke to a few minutes ago on the phone, Dana's lucky to be alive."

"What happened to her?"

"The doctor thinks it was a cocaine overdose, but he won't know for sure until the blood tests are in."

I'd never fainted in my life, yet suddenly I felt dizzy.

I closed my eyes and reached for the back of the chair for support. Tony must have noticed because he stepped closer and pulled me tight against him.

"Who's taking care of Summer?" I asked, concerned about my thirteen-year-old niece's safety. I hoped she hadn't seen her mother in that condition.

"The poor kid has been taking care of herself. I plan to catch a flight in a few hours, but I need to be close to Dana. Would you mind if Summer stayed with you for a while. A few days or a week?"

I hadn't seen my niece in years, but I remembered her childish giggle, her freckled face and her pixie hair-cut. "Wouldn't it be easier if I flew to L.A. and took care of Summer at her home?"

"I'm told your sister lives in a rough neighborhood with questionable roommates. I want my granddaughter far away from Dana's so-called friends."

"Sure, Summer can stay here until Dana feels better."

"Good, I'll call you as soon as I know more about your sister's condition and when to expect Summer's flight."

"Tell Dana not to worry. Summer can stay with me as long as she needs to."

CHAPTER 3

After two failed attempts to put the receiver back in its cradle, Tony took the phone from my trembling fingers and set it down. I told him what little I knew about my sister and my niece. Without warning, I burst into tears. He gathered me in his arms and rocked me against his solid chest.

Then he poured me a brandy and insisted I sit on the couch with my head against his shoulder. As I sipped the drink, his fingers traced slow lazy circles along my scalp, helping me to relax and finally doze off.

I awoke with a start to find the sun streaming through the slits in the closed blinds. "How long have I been asleep?"

"It's almost six." Tony yawned, freed his arm from beneath my head and stretched. "Will you be all right, or should I cancel going into work this morning?"

I appreciated his generous offer, but I knew how important the mall project was to his business. If he and his partner didn't crunch numbers this weekend, their bid wouldn't be ready by Monday. And as much as I'd have liked to have Tony with me, there was no need.

"No, I'll be fine."

He pressed a kiss to the corner of my mouth. "Are you sure? Earlier on the phone you looked ready to pass out."

"I don't know what came over me, but I'm back to my old self-reliant, tough-as-nails self."

He hugged me tight against him. "That's my Annie."

I stood and grabbed a pad of paper from the desk and started making a list: chips and dip, drinks and teen magazines.

"What will I say to her? I won't know what to do with a teenager." I drew a large exclamation point behind the word magazines.

"She'll only be here for a few days. Buy lots of pizza and plenty of junk food, set your television to MTV and don't be surprised when your phone becomes an extension of her ear," Tony said with a grin.

"She can talk on the phone all she wants... I'm sure she'll need to stay in close contact with her mom. She's my only niece, and this is my chance to help get through this difficult time. Knowing her mother's a drug addict has to be rough. I want Summer to know I'm here for her, no matter what."

To my list, I added pink bath towels for her bathroom. I suspected pretty things wouldn't lessen Summer's anguish, but I wanted to make her stay here as pleasant as possible. "I think I'll go shopping and buy a new bedspread. She can take it home with her when she leaves. Maybe I should purchase a few CDs and how about a Nintendo?"

Starting toward the bathroom, Tony threw me a teasing look over his shoulder. "There's an unwritten rule amongst teenagers to hate everything adults buy them. Why not get her a small gift for when she steps off the plane. Then make plans to go shopping together after she arrives. That way she can pick out exactly what she wants. There's another unwritten rule so you'd best be prepared—all teenagers are experts at maxing out credit cards. So be warned."

"In that case I'll bring along lots of extra cash and hire a Brink's truck to take us to the mall."

"I like the way you think," he said, disappearing into the bathroom, then poking out his head. "Depending on how long Summer stays, maybe I can persuade my daughter to show your niece around."

His daughter, Chelsea, was fourteen and very popular. Most girls would love to be part of her crowd. "That would be great. Do you think she'd be willing to do that?"

He shrugged and uttered a deep laugh. "Only if she thinks it's her idea."

I'd called Vi earlier and explained that I needed to go shopping for my niece's visit. She suggested we have lunch at the food court at the mall.

Vi slipped into the passenger seat of my Volvo. She leaned over and kissed my cheek. "I'm sorry to hear about your sister."

"Me, too, but maybe this'll make her realize she needs to make some drastic changes. I spoke to my mom this morning, and Dana is much better. My mother hopes to persuade her to go into rehab, if not for herself then for her daughter's sake."

"I'll ask Father Thompson to keep your sister in his prayers."

"If only that were all it took to turn Dana's life around."

"People change, dear," Vi reminded me.

"I hope so."

Dana had been through rehab two other times; once as a teenager, and three years ago. She'd refused to give up her friends, and within weeks of her discharge she was back to her old ways. "I'm glad you've come along because I'm going to need your help to pick out some truly special gifts for my niece. I was thinking of buying a few accessories for the bedroom she'll be using, something frilly and girlish."

"A visit with you is what that poor child needs."

As I steered my vehicle into the mall parking lot twenty minutes later, I noticed Vi's lips were pursed and her eyes filled with doubt. "What's wrong?"

"I don't know if I dare say, dear."

I parked the car and dropped my keys into my

purse. "There's nothing you can't discuss with me."
Except for Tony. Let's not ruin what little progress
we've made.

Vi glanced down, toyed with the strap of her hand-
bag. "Your niece needs to be in a stable home with an
adult she can emulate."

Her worried gray eyes met mine. "Thirteen is such
an impressionable age, and up until now, she hasn't had
a strong role model."

I sucked in my lower lip. What was she getting at?
"I plan to help Summer any way I can. I still have a few
vacation days left, and Monday I'm going to call my supervisor and explain I have a family emergency and
need to take a few days off."

"That's nice dear, but…what about Tony?"

"What about Tony?" I braced myself for what she'd
say next.

She reached over and pressed her hand over mine.
I felt a slight tremor in her fingertips. "What will that
poor child think when she discovers her aunt is living
with a man without being married? What kind of message will you be sending her?"

"These are different times and people think nothing about couples living together."

"In my day we called it shacking up."

"We don't call it that anymore."

Vi was quiet for a moment. "I won't say any more
about this matter. It's clear we'll never agree, and I

don't want to cause a greater rift between us. It's your decision to make. Be sure you aren't making a mistake."

I wonder what was best for my niece. But then, Tony had experience with girls Summer's age. He might be able to provide some insight on what I should do. In the past few months I'd grown to depend on him and value his opinion.

"I'll discuss this with Tony and see what he thinks."

True to her word, Vi didn't pursue the matter. She opened the door, swung her feet out, and threw me a brittle smile. "I'm ready to do some serious shopping. Are you?"

"You want me to move out." Tony's voice was louder than usual—close to shouting.

"No, I don't want you to go, but I'm wondering whether you'd want to leave…just while Summer is here." When he'd explained he didn't want any more children, he'd said I was free to do what I wanted but if I babysat a friend's kids, he'd make himself scarce. So I expected he'd be relieved at my offer.

"And where am I supposed to go?"

"To your house, of course."

He inhaled a ragged breath. "I didn't have time to tell you my good news yesterday. I found someone to rent my house, and my tenant moved in today."

"Oh…"

"You spend one afternoon with that old bag, and I'm already heading out the door."

I hated that he referred to Vi that way, but in a way I couldn't blame him. He'd expected her to greet him with open arms. "This has nothing to do with Vi."

"Of course it does. And that's why I'm upset. That old lady has you by the throat, and she's squeezing hard. You're an adult. You shouldn't bow down to what your ex-mother-in-law thinks is inappropriate for the kid."

The muscles in my neck cramped. "I'm worried about Summer and the influence Dana's had on her. Summer will be here for such a short while, and I want her to be able to open up. If you're here, she'll be less likely to come to me. I'm sorry. I know this isn't fair to you."

After a moment, he said a bit begrudgingly, "All right. I don't want to stand in the way of you helping your niece. This means a lot to you."

"You mean a lot to me, too, but this is an emergency. Under other circumstances, I would never ask you to go."

After a moment the hard planes of his face softened. He reached for me, rested his hands on my shoulders. "You're right, of course. Your niece needs to come first."

I wrapped my arms around his neck. "Thanks. I want Summer to get to know you."

He grinned. "You aren't afraid I'll corrupt her?"

"Never, you're a great guy, the best."

"I'm sorry if I gave you a hard time about this. Before you got here, I'd been thinking much along the same lines. Just knowing that Violet wants me out of your life put me on the defensive. I didn't want to give her the satisfaction of knowing she'd won. But this isn't about her and me. It's about your niece, and I want what's best for the kid."

"I'm glad you understand."

"I don't want to be away from you for even a few days. But I'll move out first thing tomorrow morning. When you return from the airport, I'll be gone."

"Thank you. Where will you stay?"

He sent me the crooked grin I loved. "At the Holiday Inn in Portland. That way if you decide to visit wearing a skimpy maid costume, you won't have far to drive."

This was the Tony I knew.

And loved.

"What do you think?" I asked Tony, surveying my handiwork.

"Any girl would be happy with this room." He set down the television he was carrying on the cedar chest that I'd moved against the wall across from the bed. He plugged in the portable DVD player I'd bought for Summer so she could have some privacy while she was here, especially if Tony's daughter and her friends came to visit.

I glanced at my watch again and noticed only ten minutes had elapsed. My stomach felt queasy. The last time I'd seen Summer, she'd been eight, a freckle-faced angel who giggled at everything I said. She'd squealed with delight at the doll and the tea set I'd bought her. By the way her voice had rung with excitement at doing simple things like feeding fries to the seagulls on the wooden pier at Old Orchard Beach, and playing skeet ball, and going on rides, you'd have thought she'd never been to an amusement park. But according to Dana, she had.

Summer's visit had been too short. I'd catalogued our time together under special memories and thought of my niece frequently.

What was Summer like now?

Was she into drugs?

I hoped not, but the possibility existed. What had become of the happy child left to fend for herself in the worst possible environment?

"I can't wait to see her again," I said to Tony who'd finished hauling up my purchases.

"Summer is one lucky kid to have you for an aunt."

"I hope she feels that way, too."

"Even my daughter would love these CDs. So a kid who hasn't had much of anything should be ecstatic."

"I hope so."

He took my hand and led me down the stairs into the bedroom we shared. I watched him fold a few pairs of pants and several shirts and stack them into a duffel bag he'd put on the bed. "I'm only taking a few things. Keep my side of the bed warm, I'll be back in a few days."

Vi and I arrived at the Portland Jetport half an hour early. On the second floor, a glass wall and security guards prevented us from going farther so we waited near the glass door where we'd see Summer the instant she walked through.

"Thanks for coming with me," I said.

"I wouldn't have missed it. The poor child needs lots of support. I'm here for you and for her."

I checked my watch once more. Only five minutes had gone by since the last time I'd checked.

Vi held her purse in one hand and a purple gift bag in the other, containing a small stuffed moose with the word Maine embroidered on its belly.

I carried a small brightly wrapped box tied with a red bow, which contained the charm bracelet I'd bought. I'd spent way more than I'd intended. At first I'd gone to the jewelry store wanting to buy a silver bracelet, but the gold ones had looked so much nicer. Since I only had one niece and no children of my own, I'd decided to splurge.

I hoped our gifts would help to cheer up Summer.

Some time later a group of passengers started toward the glass doors. I spotted a pretty blond girl at the same instant as Vi.

"Is that her?" Vi asked.

"I don't know." I waved a small card with the name Summer.

The girl looked at me blankly right before she was greeted by two people who could have been her parents.

I kept a watchful eye on the door. Several guys with Bates College lettermen jackets walked out, an older couple, a few businessmen with briefcases and a mother and a toddler pushing a stroller.

I'd begun to worry that something was wrong when a strange-looking girl appeared. Her short hair was dyed black with a red stripe along one side of her head. White makeup covered her face, and her eyes were ringed with black. She wore a dark, wrinkled shirt with holes at her elbows, and a black skirt that skimmed the top of scuffed army boots. Her ears, eyebrows, right nostril and her lower lip were pierced, her mouth traced in black. In her hands she carried a partially filled trash bag.

I waved the card. When she started to walk toward us, I prayed this wasn't Dana's child and instantly felt remorse.

"Summer?"

"'Fraid so."

I reminded myself to breathe. "We'll go collect your luggage."

"No need. Got everything right here," she said, indicating the plastic bag she was holding.

Vi spoke up, and I introduced them. "Summer, how nice to finally meet you," she said.

"Whatever," Summer replied.

I spotted a large silver bead on her tongue.

Reaching around her thin shoulders, I gave her a hug, but she stood stiff and unyielding.

"I was starting to worry you'd missed your flight."

"Wouldn'tcha know, I was the last one allowed to leave the plane. The dude sitting next to me said I'd stolen his wallet. Come to find out the idiot forgot he'd put it in his backpack."

CHAPTER 4

As we walked across the street and entered the parking garage, I smiled and tried to make conversation with Summer, who dragged her plastic bag along the pavement and kept her gaze riveted on her boots that looked several sizes too large.

"Are you tired, or would you like to go somewhere? The mall isn't far from here, and I have a credit card that's begging to be used."

She grunted out an impatient sound that was neither a yes nor a no. I chalked up her behavior to exhaustion—and being worried about her mother. I decided to make the most of our short while together. I'd concentrate on the positive and ignore...everything else.

If Summer were spending more time with me, I'd have loved to do something about her clothing, her hair and her makeup. Was that even makeup? Why would such a pretty child want to cover her face with white goop and outline her eyes and mouth in black?

Ghoulish.

Another pang of remorse struck me.

Summer needed my understanding, not criticism. Yet it was difficult to glance at her for even a few seconds without wanting to help transform her—to change everything from the tip of her head right down to her boot-clad feet.

I needed to accept her the way she was.

But could I?

Determined to do my best, I said, "If you're hungry, we can stop to get a bite to eat."

"That's a fine idea. I wouldn't mind stopping for a piece of pie. How does a burger and some fries sound to you?" Vi asked my niece in a hopeful tone.

Summer's downcast eyes never wavered. A moment later she gave a halfhearted shrug and bobbed her head from side to side, which I took to mean she wasn't hungry—or she might be. Since I didn't want to press the issue, I decided to offer her a sandwich once we arrived at my house.

I tucked the small box with the charm bracelet into my purse, planning to give it to her at a better time.

Would there be a better time?

Communication between us could only improve.

As we neared my Volvo, I pressed the remote to unlock the doors. I started to reach for Summer's plastic bag but her fingers tightened their grip.

"Would you like to put your things in the back?"

She shook her head and yanked the bag close to her legs as though afraid of losing her few possessions. I smiled reassuringly, but I doubt she noticed because she was too busy examining the ground by her feet.

Violet extended the gift bag beneath Summer's downcast eyes. "I bought you a welcome to Maine present."

Summer glanced warily at the package before grabbing the bag from Violet's hand, and without even glancing inside, shoved it into her plastic bag.

No "thank you" from this kid.

I admonished myself for having such petty thoughts. Summer's mother was in the hospital. I shouldn't be focusing on her appearance and poor manners.

Maybe it was a good thing I'd never been blessed with my own children. A fleeting pang of regret twisted inside.

Violet opened the front door and stepped aside so Summer could enter. "If you'd like, you can sit up front with your aunt. I don't mind the back seat."

The child hesitated. I'd expected either no reply or another shrug. Instead, Summer lifted eyes filled with contempt. "Stop trying to pretend you're both so happy to have me here." Had her voice not broken I might have missed the fear beneath the tough facade.

For a moment I saw a vulnerable little girl afraid of being hurt again, afraid of being left with strangers, afraid of being abandoned by a mother who'd let her down.

The helpless look vanished when Summer sneered. "I see right through you. Well, I'm not any happier to

45

be stuck here with you two than you are with me. I'll be out of this frigging hick state as soon as my mother comes for me. So till then, let's cut the goody-goody crap." Tears rimmed her eyes.

"Oh, Summer, you're wrong about that…." Wanting to comfort my niece, I stepped closer and reached for her shoulder, but she retreated with a warning glance. As I lowered my hand, I wondered how I'd be able to help her when she clearly didn't want me near.

Violet gasped, shock rippling over her features. "I don't mind saying your speech leaves much to be desired. You have a lot of changes to make if you ever hope to grow into a fine young lady."

"If being a fine young lady means acting like a prissy old bitch, I'll pass." Satisfaction danced in Summer's teary blue eyes as she swung her glance from Vi to me and back to Vi.

As if they had a mind of their own, the fingers of my right hand jerked up and sliced across the air. I caught myself just in time, or I'd have slapped Summer's face. I'd come damn close. Too close. Shame rushed through me. Heat rose to my cheeks.

"I'm sorry," I said. "I didn't mean that. I would never hit you."

A knowing smile curved Summer's lips. "Yeah, right."

Violet's jaw hung open for a moment before she snapped her mouth shut and slid onto the front seat.

I knew Summer had chosen her words for shock value.

She'd succeeded.

She'd insulted Violet.

More important, *what was wrong with me?* Until now, I'd never come close to hitting anyone. I'd have a long talk with Summer later. That way I wouldn't be reprimanding her in front of Vi. Then I'd apologize to her again for losing control. Maybe I could persuade her to apologize to Vi.

Like that was going to happen any time soon.

I sent Vi a rueful look. She patted my hand and whispered, "Don't worry about it, dear."

A new wave of shame washed over me as I realized I couldn't wait for Summer to leave.

Summer's stony gaze pierced right through me as she scooted into the back seat and slammed the door.

I longed for the sweet young girl she'd been and the closeness we'd shared years ago.

I rounded the front of my car and slipped inside. No one spoke as I maneuvered the vehicle onto the Maine Turnpike and twenty minutes later took the Gray exit. I dropped off my mother-in-law first. As I continued toward home, I could hear Summer sniffing behind me. In the rearview mirror, I watched her wipe away tears from her face with the back of her hand. Trails of pale flesh crisscrossed her thick white makeup. Summer resembled a young child at Halloween, who'd discovered too late that her bag of candy had a hole in it.

If only her problems were that simple.

No matter what Summer said or did, I'd be patient with her. Surely I could handle being with my niece for a few days.

I vowed again to do my best to look beneath the surface and find the child I remembered.

And loved.

Tony's Porsche pulled into my driveway three hours later. Relieved to see him stroll up my walk, I opened the door and rushed outside to meet him. My cardigan sweater fluttered in the cool evening breeze. As I reached up to brush a dark strand of hair that had fallen over his forehead, he pulled me against him. My arms circling his neck, I absorbed his warmth and his strength, my pent-up emotions and stress forgotten for a moment as his mouth came down on mine.

"How about we slip into the back seat of my car for a quickie," he murmured against my lips.

I chuckled. "There's no backseat."

"I'll make do."

"I bet you would." I moved away and, taking his hand, led him inside the house. "Thanks for coming over. I could really use some advice."

"Has your niece come out of the bedroom yet?"

"No, not even to eat supper." I worried my lower lip, not caring that my bad habit showed lack of confidence. When it came to Summer, I had no idea what to do, what to say, how to act.

Tony released my hand and wrapped his arm around my shoulder. "She'll come down when she's hungry enough."

"I guess so. How's your room at the motel?"

"Nothing special. Thankfully it's only for a few days."

"A few days could be a very long time. I'm in way over my head. What do I know about talking to a teenager?"

He kissed the tip of my nose. "You'll do fine, and if you have any questions, I'm only a phone call away. Also, I spoke to Chelsea. She thinks hanging out with someone from Los Angeles would be cool."

"That's great." *If nothing else it would give me some time away from Summer.* Guilt flowed through me. If they gave out an award for the worst aunt of the year, the trophy would be sitting on my mantel.

Tony crossed the room and opened the glass door to the cabinet where I stored a few bottles of wine and brandy. "Would you like a glass?"

"Sure."

He poured white merlot into two glasses and after handing me one, sat on the couch. I lowered myself next to him.

"How did you get your daughter to agree?" I asked.

"I told Chelsea I'd finance a shopping spree to the mall if she volunteered to introduce your niece to her friends tomorrow after school."

In our short phone conversation, I hadn't had a

chance to explain that Summer was…well…a bit different. "Summer wears a lot of makeup," I said, realizing this was an understatement.

He shrugged nonchalantly. "So does Chelsea…when her mom isn't looking. The last time I picked Chelsea up she looked like a raccoon with her eyes lined in black."

"She wears heavy army type boots." *Probably to kick the butts of unsuspecting old ladies.*

Tony laughed. "You worry too much. All teenagers experiment with clothing. For months last year my daughter wouldn't go out the door without her oversized camouflage jacket she'd purchased for two bucks at Goodwill. She resembled an emaciated hunter."

Was Tony right? Was I overreacting?

"How about I sneak back in tonight after everyone's asleep?" he asked, kissing the side of my face.

I knew he was joking, but the idea was appealing. "I'm tempted. What would you say if I asked you to get your suitcase and move back in tonight?"

"I'd be a selfish cold-hearted bastard not to give you the time you need with your niece."

I'm sure he was right. Yet I was disappointed because he hadn't jumped at the opportunity.

"Hey, why the frown?"

Before I could reply, I heard a commotion in the backyard and the sound of splintering wood. I dashed outside with Tony at my heels to find Summer scrambling to her feet, the trellis that had been secured to the side of the house in pieces on the ground, several vines to my climbing roses torn.

"Are you all right?" I asked, hurrying to her side, reaching for her.

Summer flinched away. "Yup." She lifted her long skirt and brushed dirt off her black nylons, which had holes in the knees.

In the dim light I saw that she'd applied a fresh layer of white makeup.

"What happened?" I asked.

"Isn't it obvious?"

Instead of using the door like a normal person, she'd tried to climb down the trellis. Where was she going? Was she running away? Since I didn't spot her black plastic bag, I assumed she'd planned to climb back up later.

"Oh, this is Tony," I said and saw the disbelief on his face. My stomach twisted nervously.

After a pause, his mouth curved into a crooked grin.

Much to my surprise Summer smiled back. "Is that your set of wheels out front?"

"Yes."

"That's cool."

"Thanks."

"Can I start her up?"

Silence followed.

Indecision streaked across Tony's face.

"That's Tony's pride and joy," I said. I understood his

reluctance, yet I was still a bit irritated that he hadn't replied yet.

She waved a hand weighed down with rings. Blunt, black polished fingernails sliced through the air. "I don't care anyway."

But she did. And because of that it mattered to me, too.

"Well," I said with my best smile directed at Tony. "Hand over the keys so Summer and I can listen to the purr of the engine."

"An engine like that wouldn't purr. It would growl, right Tony?" Summer added. "So can I start her up?"

For a moment, I thought he'd refuse.

He dug in his pocket and threw her the keys. "Be gentle."

Her fingers swiped the keys, and she threw him another smile. "Cool."

In that instant I loved Tony more than I'd thought possible. If he'd asked me to marry him, I'd have agreed.

Until now, Summer had dragged her feet when she walked. She ran past me and raced through the house, the heels of her heavy boots thumping on the hardwood floor, as she dashed out the front door. I'd barely caught up with her and dropped into the passenger seat when the engine roared to life.

From the doorway, I spotted a worried Tony watching our every move. I couldn't blame him, but relinquishing his keys had been the ultimate sacrifice. I appreciated what he'd done, and I'd certainly tell him so later.

"This is the coolest car I've ever sat in." Summer turned on the CD player and immediately shut it off, silencing Tim McGraw. "How can anyone stand listening to that crap?"

I liked country music, but I wasn't about to admit to such depravity. This was as close as I'd come to having a civil conversation with Summer. "That music isn't so bad."

Summer rolled her eyes. "If I had a car like this, I'd be the most popular kid in L.A." She fiddled with the radio until she found a heavy metal station and turned up the volume so loud I felt the bass pulsating around me.

"Do you think he'd mind if I backed it up a few inches in the driveway?"

Tony had left the doorway and stood near his car, wringing his hands.

"Mind? He'd go crazy."

She threw me a knowing glance and laughed, her smile directed at me.

My heart skipped a beat. She'd let down her guard, and I hoped that was a sign of good things to come.

"I'd sure love to take it around the block," she said, wistfully.

"Maybe if you had a permit."

"Yeah, as if."

"You're right." *If it were my car, I'd let her.*

A moment later Summer turned off the ignition, swung the door open and threw Tony his keys. "Thanks."

She'd thanked him.

More progress.

"I was thinking of heading out for pizza. Would you like some?" he asked.

"Sure, can I come?"

He threw me a questioning glance, and I nodded approvingly.

"Only if you promise not to play your music," he said, a strained, crooked grin in place.

They returned some time later with two large pizzas, a liter of Pepsi and a bag of vinegar chips. I knew instantly that something was wrong.

Tony slammed the boxes down on the counter and disappeared into the bathroom.

Summer took a paper plate I'd set on the table, loaded it with pizza and chips.

"Mmmm-mmm, vinegar chips are my favorite," I said, taking one from the bag.

She rolled her eyes, shrugged, poured herself a glass of Pepsi and, grabbing her plate, charged up the stairs. At least she wouldn't starve.

She'd no sooner slammed the bedroom door shut when Tony entered the kitchen.

"What happened?" I asked.

"That kid has a fresh mouth."

Tell me something I don't already know. "She's had a rough life."

"That's no excuse for her to call me an uptight prick."

Here I'd thought we were making progress. "Why'd she say that?"

"Because she wanted to?"

Which didn't tell me a thing.

Not that I'd have taken Summer's side, but I needed to understand. Should I press for details or wait until he'd calmed down?

I wrapped my arms around his waist. "She's here for only a few days. I need you two to get along."

His voice softened. "I'll try, but that might not be possible."

Though disappointed, I appreciated his honesty. "What set her off?"

His muscles tensed under my touch. "Are you taking sides?"

"No, just trying to understand."

"There's no understanding that kid. She's rude. It's as simple as that."

"What were you talking about when she got upset?"

Tony pulled away, walked toward the sink and poured himself a tall glass of water. He drank half, turned and leaned against the granite countertop. "I was trying to get through to her, but she wasn't having any of it. I told her how much work you'd done to make her stay special. The least she could do is show a little appreciation and not give you a hard time."

"I don't need you fighting my battles."

"I know that. I was only trying to help."

"Is that when she called you—"

"She didn't say a word, instead she stared blankly out the window. Before I went inside to get the pizza, she asked if I could leave the engine running so she could listen to the radio. Of course I refused. I was afraid to come out and find her gone."

"I certainly understand."

"When I returned a moment later with the food, she was hunched against the seat, pouting. Thinking it would make her feel better, I pointed out that no one but me drives the Porsche. Not even you."

That news didn't settle well. "Does this mean you wouldn't let me drive your car if I asked?"

"No, of course not."

But there was enough doubt in his tone to make me wonder.

"So when exactly did Summer start calling you names?"

"Right after she found out you'd never driven my Porsche."

"It sounds as though you think more of that damn car than me."

"I never knew you wanted to drive my Porsche."

"I didn't…but now I do. Very much."

"Then let's go for a spin."

This was silly. I really didn't care about driving his car. *It was the principle.*

Plus it had a stick, and I was no good at shifting. *I had to be sure he trusted me with his precious car.*

He took his keys and slapped them into my palm.

I had my answer. I grabbed the keys, but after a few seconds, I handed them back to him.

He shook his head. "I thought we were going for a ride."

"I just needed to know you'd let me drive your Porsche. I feel better now."

When he nabbed the keys, his fingers captured mine. "Nothing is more important to me than you."

"Not even your Porsche?"

"Let me think about that for a minute," he said with a teasing grin.

I reciprocated with an elbow to his ribs. But it was all in jest. Because he'd proven to me that I mattered most.

Still, I couldn't help but wonder—would he still have been smiling if I'd really taken his pride and joy for a ride?

We sat and ate pizza, discussed my job and his. He wouldn't know for another week whether his firm got the bid for the mall. It was almost midnight when he stood to leave. I walked him to the door and leaned against him.

We held each other and kissed.

"Last chance for that quickie in the back of my car," he whispered into my ear.

I sighed. "There's not enough room."

A deep sexy laugh rumbled from his chest. "Where there's a will, there's a way."

CHAPTER 5

Around midnight, wearing my comfy flannel nightgown and slippers, I crept up the stairs and listened outside my niece's bedroom. Silence. My gut wrenched. Was Summer sleeping or had she escaped through the window?

How would I explain to my mother that I'd lost her granddaughter?

As I imagined all sorts of gruesome possibilities, I pushed the door open and was relieved to see her curled up in bed. I tiptoed across the room. The light from the bathroom slanted across the bed. I saw wet bath towels on the tiled floor beside the tub.

Typical teenager. Didn't pick up after herself.

This revelation gave me hope.

Along with the fact she'd removed her makeup and looked less intimidating. She sighed softly. I wanted to sit next to Summer and take her into my arms. But I didn't dare wake her.

Such a pretty girl.

Yet so confused.

As I admired her long eyelashes sweeping her tear-streaked face, I noticed her right hand curled under her chin, fingers clutching the little moose Vi had given her. I spotted part of a plastic bag sticking out from under the sheets and the ribbed neck of the oversized bright yellow nightgown I'd bought for her.

When I'd picked Summer up at the airport, I instantly regretted purchasing the nightgown and had never expected her to wear it.

A child of contradictions.

I'd also selected several T-shirts, which were no longer on the bureau. Had she tucked those into her bag? Compassion swelled in my chest for my niece who felt she had to guard her possessions.

I bent and brushed my lips against her cheek that smelled like Ivory soap. I considered turning off the bathroom light but remembered that at eight years old, she'd insisted on leaving a light on while she slept.

Summer put up a tough front, but inside, I suspected she was still a frightened little girl.

I'd need to remember that tomorrow, if confronted by the angry teenager clad in black, her face masked in white.

The next morning, determined to get reacquainted with my niece, I jumped out of bed, threw on jeans, a T-shirt and slid my feet into my slippers. I called my supervisor and explained I'd need some time off due to a family emergency. Once I'd taken care of that, I checked with the hospital to see how my sister was doing. The nurse in charge let me speak to my mom.

"Hi, how's Dana?"

"She's doing much better, but she's suffering from malnutrition."

"Will she be all right?"

"The doctor says she's had a close call. She might not be so lucky next time."

"I wish I could be there with her."

"I know that, dear. How's Summer?"

"She's still sleeping. We had a bit of a rough start yesterday, but I'm certain we're going to get along fine."

"That's a relief. Say hi to her for me."

"Will do."

"What's the phone number to Dana's room? The woman at the switchboard wouldn't give it to me. I'm sure Summer will want to talk to her when she wakes up." I'd hoped speaking to her mom would ease Summer's worries, and maybe lessen the strain between us.

"To be perfectly honest, Dana doesn't want to deal with Summer right now. Your sister needs to focus on herself and getting well. I hope you understand."

I didn't. "Dana has focused on herself for her entire adult life.

My mother issued a low groan. "Don't be too hard on your sister. She has her faults, but right now, she needs our support and understanding."

My sister needed someone to kick her butt, but we'd never agree. "Tell Dana that Summer and I send our love."

"I'll do that. I'll call you tomorrow. Take care."

"You, too. Bye."

I hurried into the kitchen and took down the pancake mix from the cupboard, measured out two cups into a bowl and added milk and eggs. I took out my frustration by beating the mixture by hand. I knew that Dana was weak, but I couldn't understand her not wanting to talk to her own daughter. It was the epitome of selfishness. Not only had Dana chosen drugs over Summer, but she'd also turned her back on her child when Summer needed her the most.

The scrape of heavy boots against the tile floor heralded Summer's arrival.

I turned to greet her. "Good morning."

She'd hidden her face with white makeup and painted tiny black stars at the corners of her eyes lined with black. I inhaled a fortifying deep breath. Nothing today would mar my good, positive mood. Well, except for Dana's selfishness. Today I'd break the hardened shell Summer had erected around herself. Today we'd become friends.

Picturing the lost little girl I'd seen curled in bed last night, I gave her a bright smile. "I just got off the phone with your grandma. Your mom is feeling much better this morning, but she has strict orders to rest so we can't call her. Maybe tomorrow you'll be able to talk to her."

"Whatever," Summer said, waving her hand, her frown deepening.

"I'm sure your mom misses you a great deal."

She shrugged. Disbelieving eyes met mine.

I'd expected Summer to vent her anger over not being able to speak to her mom. Was she disappointed? Maybe after everything she'd been through, she didn't want to talk to Dana.

Hoping to change the subject and boost Summer's mood, I asked, "Would you like blueberries in your pancakes or do you prefer them plain?"

She lowered her head. "You don't need to go to all that bother. Coffee will do."

What kind of breakfast was that for a growing child? Did she skip breakfast most mornings? "It's no bother. I like to cook."

"Yeah, right. I hope you don't expect me to do the dishes and all that cleaning up shit."

I winced at her language. "I hate doing dishes, too. That's why I have a dishwasher."

A look of satisfaction claimed her face as she shrugged and dropped into a chair.

I remembered Tony's conversation with her, and I didn't want Summer to consider herself a burden. "I might have gone a little overboard on preparing for your arrival because I was so excited. I had such a good time shopping that I couldn't stop myself, so if you don't like something, feel free to say so. I only wish you were here under happier circumstances. After your mom's better, I hope you can come see me every few months."

She lifted her right shoulder in a noncommittal shrug.

I tried a new subject. "Oh, Tony's daughter, Chelsea, is about your age. She's invited you to hang out with her and her friends at the mall this afternoon."

"Why'd she want to do that?" she asked, suspicion darkening her eyes.

"She thought it would be cool to hang out with someone from L.A."

"Oh."

I'd expected her to refuse. *Oh* sounded promising. "So will you go?"

"Maybe." Her lips twitched, a smile tugging the corners of her mouth.

More progress.

"I'll give you fifty bucks."

"You don't need to do that."

"I want to. The other girls will want to shop for clothes, and I thought you would, too."

"I got plenty of clothes."

That was a matter of opinion.

Why was I so judgmental around Summer?

Because I cared, deeply. "You can still take the cash

in case you find a CD or something else you can't live without."

Her wary gaze met mine. "What do you want from me in exchange?"

"I want you to have a good time while you're here."

"Yeah, right."

"I mean it. Do you remember how much fun we had the last time you were here?"

A faraway look came into her eyes. "No."

Disappointed, I forced a smile. "I'm surprised you don't remember, we had such a great time."

Directing a stony gaze at me, she said nothing.

I glanced down and adjusted the dial on the electric frying pan. "So what'll it be, plain or blueberry pancakes?"

"Can I have some of both?"

"Coming right up."

A few minutes later I placed a stack of pancakes on a plate in the center of the table along with a half gallon of milk and two glasses of orange juice. I poured myself a cup of coffee and sat in the chair nearest Summer. "Help yourself."

She slid three pancakes onto her plate.

I took two and handed her the syrup.

She drenched her pancakes and put a large bite into her mouth. She polished off her serving before I'd eaten half of mine.

"Can I have those, too?" she asked, her fork poised over the dish.

"They're there to eat."

Needing no more encouragement, Summer ate the last few pancakes. Some time later she wiped her mouth with the paper napkin beside her plate. "I lied to you earlier. I do remember the last time I was here. We had a blast."

Her comment took me off guard. "We certainly did."

"I ran after the seagulls when they stole my bag of cookies," she said with a giggle that reminded me of the child she'd been.

"I have a picture on my mantel of you feeding the gulls French fries on the pier."

"I noticed it when I first arrived. I was surprised you still had it."

I reached for her hand, and she didn't pull away. "I've missed you."

"Yeah, well…" She looked uneasy and unsure how to reply.

We'd made progress.

Hope blossomed inside me.

I wanted to tell her how much I cared and worried about her. But Summer freed her hand and frowned, the closeness between us vanishing.

I wanted Summer's outing with Chelsea to go well. But I was concerned about my niece's ability to pepper most sentences with obscenities. I had no idea how to broach the subject without causing us to drift further apart.

But I had to try.

Later that day I knocked on Summer's bedroom door. "Can I come in?"

"Suit yourself. It's your house."

I walked into the bedroom and saw Summer standing with her back to me, her plastic bag on the bed, some of its contents spread out in front of her—most of the clothing black with the exception of the few T-shirts I'd purchased. Summer wore a black skirt that reached midcalf, ripped fishnet stockings, the same clunky boots and a black long-sleeve shirt with holes in the elbows.

My heart fell toward my stomach like a rock. What did I expect? Summer in a prom gown?

Accept her as she is.

Easier said than done.

How would Chelsea and her friends react when they first saw Summer? Chelsea was a cute girl, five foot five, straight brown hair that brushed her shoulders. She often wore low-slung jeans and cropped tops that showed off her pierced belly button.

When Summer turned, I was pleased to see she'd removed most of the white from her face. She'd left behind a thin layer that made her look deathly pale, but the hint of flesh tone was there.

Under her shirt I spotted a wedge of the pink top I'd bought poking from the unbuttoned collar. The bright color reflected a rosy glow against her chin.

"You look nice," I said.

She glanced down and shrugged, seemingly uncomfortable with the compliment. Around her wrists she wore thick leather bracelets with metal prongs. I thought of the charm bracelet in my purse and realized how out of place it would look on her.

"I'll be right back," I said, running down the stairs, fetching the box from my purse, and heading back into Summer's room.

"I bought this for you because I had one when I was your age. But I know it isn't your style. While you're at the mall, you can return it for something you like."

She took the box and looked down at the package for a long time.

"Aren't you going to open it?"

Her gaze strayed across the room. "I saw you ditch this yesterday when you saw what I looked like. I figured you were disappointed."

"I was a little surprised," I said with a nervous laugh. "Well, make that a lot surprised."

She rolled her eyes.

"And of course, you've changed…a lot." *Keep it up and she'll be escaping out the window.*

"You think I'm a freak."

I winced at her choice of words. I exhaled a long

breath. "No, you aren't a freak, but I don't know what to think," I finally said.

"At least you're honest," she replied, her gaze riveted on me.

"We don't have many Goth teens around here. Isn't that what you are? A Goth?"

"I'm just me, that's all."

"I understand that you want to express yourself, and that's fine. I've gotten over my initial surprise, and I hope you've forgiven me for raising my hand at you."

"No big deal."

"But to me it's a very big deal."

I waited a moment for her reaction.

Another shrug.

"I didn't give you this yesterday because I realized I should have listened to Tony and waited for you to pick out your own gift."

Summer frowned at the mention of his name but kept her thoughts to herself. She slid the ribbon over the rounded edges of the wrapped velvet box, slowly removed the wrapping, folded the paper, and tucked it into her plastic bag along with the ribbon and the bow. She flipped the box open and stared down at the gold charm bracelet.

"I know this is a sad time for you, but I figured there was no reason why we couldn't make some special memories while you were here." I'd hoped she'd look back at our time together in a good way. I'd planned to buy her other charms over the years.

Her gaze locked with mine.

"You probably think the gift is foolish, and I don't blame you." I was rambling and couldn't seem to stop. "As I said earlier, exchange it for something you like."

She lifted and dropped her shoulders and studied the bracelet.

Summer raised doubt-filled eyes.

"The seagull charm was supposed to remind you of the great time we had together when you were eight."

"I already figured that." She shrugged and glanced at the bracelet again. "Can you help me put it on?"

I was pleased and discovered a moment later that it didn't look nearly as out of place as I'd expected, dangling beneath the thick leather band around her wrist.

She jiggled her wrist and watched the charm sway back and forth, her eyes sparkling with joy.

"It looks really pretty on you," I said.

"No shit, it's the prettiest thing I've ever owned."

I sensed her enthusiasm and a growing bond between us.

Unfortunately, I now had to ask Summer to tone down her language. I'd considered not saying anything and allowing the girls to relate to each other, but I feared Summer wouldn't fit in. And if my small pep talk might avert a potential disaster, then I had to give it a try.

But I dreaded Summer's response.

CHAPTER 6

"We need to talk," I said, hoping Summer would understand I wanted the best for her.

She frowned. Tears gathered in the corners of her eyes. "Is it about my mom?"

"No, if I'd heard anything, I'd have told you right away. This is about you going to the mall with Chelsea and her friends."

"If they've blown me off, it's not a big deal." Her anxious tone said otherwise.

"They haven't changed their minds. It's just that I want you to have a good time, but…" How to phrase this without insulting her? I bit down on my lower lip and inhaled slowly. "I'm hoping you'll get along with the girls, but I'm concerned about your language."

Her penciled black eyebrows angled sharply. "What the hell's wrong with the way I talk?"

"You need to clean it up a little. At times, the words you choose are offensive, especially to adults. I certainly don't want to tell you how to speak with kids your age."

Which was exactly what I was trying to do. Damn, I was bad at parenting.

"Just have a great time and don't worry about what I've said. I'm sure you'll do fine." Yet I wasn't sure. The few times I'd met Chelsea she'd seemed rather innocent, her manners refined. I leaned closer, intending to touch Summer's shoulder to show my support.

She stepped back, the look in her eyes warning me to keep my distance. "Don't worry, I won't embarrass you."

I lowered my hand and forced myself to smile. "I just want this to be a good experience. I'd hate for you to be disappointed."

"It sure as hell wouldn't be the first time."

When Tony arrived a short time later, I was surprised to see his Porsche in my driveway. When he took his daughter and her friends to the mall, he'd leave his car behind and use his extended cab Ford pickup.

"Hey, babe," he said, wrapping his arms around me, his lips brushing against mine.

"Where's Chelsea?"

"She went home sick from school."

"When did you find this out?"

A strange look flashed across his face. "Late morning, I think."

"Why didn't you call to tell me then?"

"I didn't think of it, sorry."

"Will Chelsea be all right?"

"Kids bounce back quickly."

"Summer will be so disappointed." She'd removed most of her white makeup. I'd hoped because she wanted to fit in.

"That's life," he said, much too casually.

"This was important to Summer. It was a chance for her to try to forget about her troubles for a few hours."

"We'll make it up to her by taking her out to eat."

I doubted that would amount to the same thing. "She was looking forward to being with kids her age. So what's wrong with Chelsea?"

I had this gut feeling, hoped I was wrong. Was he lying to me? Yet the guilt was there in his eyes, as easy to read as the headlines on a newspaper.

He looked uncomfortable, waited a moment before replying. "Errr… I think it's the flu or maybe that time of the month."

My insides clenched with anger.

And disappointment.

"You aren't telling me the truth, are you?"

He shook his head, looked as though he were going to deny it before glancing down. When he looked up, his expression was that of a small boy caught in a lie. "All right, you got me."

"Got you, is that all you can say?" I stepped away from him. Was there something wrong with me that I picked men with an aversion to the truth? He knew how I felt about lies.

"Take it easy, babe."

"Don't tell me to take it easy. I despise lies, and you know it."

"I didn't want to hurt your feelings. But if it's the truth you want, here it is. Chelsea isn't sick. I don't want my daughter hanging around with Summer."

I wondered what choice words had run through his mind before he settled on her name.

"Look at the kid," he said. "She's strange, and I won't subject Chelsea to that. Summer could be on drugs for all you know. Surely, you can see my side."

Part of me understood what he was saying. But the part of me that had seen the light in Summer's eyes when I'd mentioned the outing, didn't want to understand. "My niece doesn't need another disappointment in her life. And I doubt she would have corrupted Chelsea in one afternoon."

He exhaled a long exasperated breath. "It's not a chance I'm willing to take. You're in this so deep you don't see the entire picture." He lowered his tone and pointed toward the stairway. "I don't understand what would make a kid want to look like that. But…even though I love you, I need to look out for what I think is best for Chelsea. Don't let this come between us. I'm sorry about lying to you. I did it for you…because I didn't want to hurt you."

"You lied because you were too much of a coward to tell me the truth."

"Ouch," he said, jerking his head as though I'd slapped him. He paused a moment, his gaze sincere. "But I deserved that." He moved close and pulled me against him.

As much as I hated to think of how disappointed Summer would be, I knew Tony was doing what he thought best for his daughter. I couldn't fault him for that.

"I hope this is the last time you lie to me."

He rested his forehead against mine. "It'll never happen again. You have my word."

I asked Tony to leave so I could spend time alone with Summer. He'd agreed a bit too quickly, like someone freeing his neck from a noose. As he went out the door, he offered to pick up some Chinese food for us. But I refused because I wanted to take my niece out to eat.

I watched him climb into his car, wave and drive away. I then went upstairs to give Summer the bad news.

I knocked.

"What's up?"

I opened the door, stepped inside and noticed Summer had taken off the bright pink top from under her black shirt. She'd applied a thicker layer of white makeup and had painted tiny lines around her eyes that angled down and made her look incredibly sad.

"There's been a change in plans. Chelsea isn't coming over."

"No shit. I figured that out when Tony arrived alone."

"If you'd like, the two of us will head to the mall, do some shopping and grab a bite to eat."

"Whatever, I didn't want to be with those prissy girls, anyway. I didn't expect Chelsea to show. What lame excuse did she come up with?"

I probably should have anticipated that question, but I hadn't. I needed to lead by example. If nothing else, I had to be true to my word, even if those words might hurt Summer.

"Tony doesn't know you like I do, and well, some people have a tendency to judge others by the way they look. I think we can both agree that your style isn't something we're used to around here."

"He was afraid I'd turn his precious daughter into a thief or something?"

"Possibly, but as I said, he doesn't know you like I do."

"Anyway, it doesn't matter."

"It does to me," I said. "What do you say you and I go on a serious shopping spree?"

"Can I go just like this, or do you expect me to jump through hoops for you?"

At first I wasn't sure what she meant, but after a moment I knew she was asking whether I'd allow her to go as she was. I was tempted to ask her to remove some of her makeup. But that would only prove I didn't accept her.

Which apparently was still a fact.

Guilt washed over me. I was a poor excuse for an aunt.

"You're welcome to join me just the way you are," I finally said and watched her shoulders sag with relief.

The phone rang and as I hurried to answer it, I glanced over my shoulder. "We'll leave in about an hour?"

She lifted one shoulder in a noncommittal shrug.

I dashed downstairs and picked up the receiver.

"Annie, it's Vi. It's urgent I meet with you right away."

"What's wrong?"

"I've done some research about Goth teenagers, which you should see."

"Can this wait until tomorrow? I promised Summer we'd go to the mall."

"This will only take a few minutes. I'll be right over."

I made a pot of coffee and waited. Vi's maroon Buick pulled into my driveway a few minutes later.

Vi entered my kitchen and threw a manila folder on the table. "I'm concerned about that child upstairs." She draped her coat over a chair. "I'll only be here a few minutes so don't bother hanging it up."

I stirred a spoon of sugar and a dollop of cream into her cup. I left my coffee black, and sat in the chair opposite Vi. "So what's up?"

"I went online and looked up Goth teens, and what I learned alarmed me." She lowered her voice. "Are you certain Summer is in her room because I don't want her to hear this."

I stood and peeked into the living room. Seeing no sign of my niece, I sat back down and waited for Vi to continue.

"It's all right here in this folder. I printed everything out. There's a lot more going on in the Goth culture than applying white makeup with a spatula and looking ghoulish. Your niece may need professional help. I'm willing to help you foot the bill."

"She's only going to be here for a few days. There isn't time for her to go into therapy." How could I help Summer? She certainly didn't trust me enough to open up and discuss how she felt.

"Then you'd better keep a close eye on the child. According to what I learned, Goth teens have a fascination with death. They have a high suicide rate. Look at this," she said, flipping the folder open and pointing midpage. "Young people turn to the Goth culture because they feel alienated from society. They don't belong."

I skimmed the information in the pages she'd brought over. A chill raced down my spine. "I don't see how I can help her in such a short time. Plus, just because she dresses Goth doesn't mean she thinks Goth. Maybe she just likes to dress up and look different."

"It's possible, but you should make it clear to your

sister that she needs to act now. A trained therapist will know how to speak to Summer and find out what's going on. I'm willing to help her pay for the help Summer needs."

"That's very generous of you, but—"

"There are no buts about it. I want to help. I know how important Summer is to you, and I can easily afford to do this."

For a moment I contemplated what I'd just learned. "I can't look at Summer without wondering what's going on in her head. I suspect this is her way of coping with her mother's neglect."

"I'm sure that's a big part of her problem," Vi said.

"If I could, I'd transform Summer into a normal thirteen-year-old girl."

"I suspect that somewhere under all that makeup is a sweet thirteen-year-old child crying out for help."

Tears sprang into my eyes. A sweet thirteen-year-old child—finally someone who felt as I did. "Thanks for saying that."

"I mean it. I know kids. I didn't spend thirty-five years teaching seventh grade because of the money. I wanted to make a difference."

"Once Dana is released from the hospital, I'll tell her about our conversation and that we're willing to pay for Summer to go into counseling. But there's no guarantee my sister will go along with this." I paused; a helpless feeling came over me. "And even if Dana agrees, we'll have no way of knowing she's using our money as we intended."

Smiling, Vi lifted her hand and waved her index finger. "I've already thought of that. If Dana agrees, we'll send our payment directly to the therapist." Vi took a sip of coffee and placed the delicate cup in front of her.

I preferred mugs, but whenever Vi visited, I used the fine china with tiny painted pink roses she'd bought as a wedding gift.

"Is Tony helping you with Summer?" she asked.

A disappointed feeling settled in my chest. Tony had let me down. Maybe not deliberately, but I'd expected him to support me emotionally. "He's moved out for a few days so that Summer and I can have some alone time."

"That's probably for the best." A pained expression slipped over her face. "After Summer leaves, I plan to invite you and Tony to my house for dinner, that's if you two want to come over."

A weight lifted from my shoulders.

Just as I'd hoped, Vi was ready to accept Tony. It was time for him to stop calling her *that old bag*. "I'll check with him and get back to you."

CHAPTER 7

Summer decided she wasn't interested in going to the mall so I ordered Chinese food, and we ate in front of the television. My niece flicked through the channels and paused for a moment to watch reruns of the *Waltons* on the cable channel.

Some time later she threw back her head and laughed. "What a bunch of crap."

Thinking I'd missed something, I asked, "What?"

She waved her hand around, her mouth forming a wry smile. "This show's a joke. All this lovey, dovey, family-marriage crap is crazy."

"I'm sure no one could measure up to the Waltons, but I bet some families and marriages come close."

"Yeeeeah, right." Her expression turned sullen. A glint came into her eyes. "I'm surprised you feel like that."

"Why wouldn't I?"

"According to my mom, your husband was humping everyone in a skirt. She never understood why you didn't kick his sorry ass out the door."

I felt the color drain from my face.

Her words bombarded me, and for several seconds, I couldn't speak. Even Dana had known about Paul's infidelity. Who'd told her? Relatives or friends? Since we were both raised in this area, it could be either. Bad news sure traveled fast. Why hadn't I suspected? Was I the only one unaware that Paul was cheating on me? My stomach churned.

And Summer knew. I was embarrassed to face her.

Eighteen long months, and Paul's betrayal hurt as much as the day I'd found out. Would I ever get rid of the hollow ache inside? Would I ever be able to completely trust another man?

I trusted Tony.

But not enough to marry him.

That decision had been mutual. But I'd cheered him on when he'd downgraded the institution of marriage.

Humping everyone in a skirt.

How degrading to hear this from my niece.

As ugly as the truth of Paul's cheating had been, Summer's choice of words angered me, put me on the defensive. I stood and started to leave the room, then decided to confront her so I turned. "This is an inappropriate conversation for a thirteen-year-old to have with her aunt," I said, my voice brittle and harsh. "And I want you to clean up the way you talk to me."

"Yeah, well, sooorrrry." Her disbelieving eyes pierced

me. "I was just proving my point. I'm never gonna get married, and I sure as hell won't ever have any kids."

She jumped up and started toward the stairs.

In truth I was glad to see her leave. I didn't want to face the child who'd so bluntly pointed out the state of my marriage. Yet she'd barely eaten. I was the adult. I needed to act like an adult instead of an emotional wreck. I'd harnessed my emotions since the day I'd learned about Paul's women.

"Summer, please come back and finish your meal. I didn't mean to raise my voice, but you took me off guard." *An understatement.* She'd knocked me on my behind. Of course Summer would have chosen a more colorful word.

She turned stony eyes toward me. "Anyway, I'm tired, so I'm going to bed. And don't bother making pancakes tomorrow because they suck."

She stomped up the stairs and slammed the door.

I slept little that night. And when I dozed, I saw Paul's face, heard his words of love. For a while, I savored his kisses, but when I looked into his eyes, I saw another woman's reflection.

I awoke with a start and sat up in bed, my pulse pounding in my ears. What had I done wrong? Maybe if I'd been a better wife, he'd have been faithful.

Don't go there again.

I'd stopped blaming myself months ago.

"I've moved on," I whispered, gaining strength from the words.

Earlier Summer had been rude and thoughtless, but I shouldn't have shouted at her for repeating what she'd heard. We'd both been wrong, but I was the adult, expected to lead by good example. If I couldn't control my anger, how could I expect Summer to?

I slid my feet into my slippers and went upstairs to check on my niece. Vi's conversation earlier that day worried me. I knew Summer needed counseling, but I doubted Dana would agree.

When I pushed the door open, I saw the bed was empty. I inhaled a shaky breath and held it. If Summer had run off, I'd never forgive myself. What did I know about teenagers?

Especially one with emotional problems.

Then I heard sniffing. I saw her sitting on the floor in the corner of the room, her knees pulled up to her chest, her arms wrapped tight around her legs. In the dim light slanting through the partially opened bathroom door I saw her, hugging the tiny moose Vi had given her.

I moved the plastic trash bag that held her possessions, dropped down beside her and put my arms around her thin frame.

"Leave me alone," she said between sobs.

But she didn't push me away so I continued to hold her. "Summer, what's wrong?"

"Everything."

As she cried, I rubbed my hand over her back and kissed the top of her head. She smelled like soap and shampoo. The scent reminded me of Summer's last visit, when she was eight and a happy child, when we'd cuddled on the couch and watched cartoons together. But even back then I'd seen signs of neglect. Why hadn't I done something? But what? When I'd questioned Dana, she'd assured me Summer was on the right track, a busy child doing well in school.

A shudder racked her body. "My mom's right. I'm a mean bitch, and I don't know when to keep my mouth shut."

Rage surged inside me. How could Dana call her own daughter a bitch? My sister didn't deserve to be a mother.

"Everyone says things they don't mean once in a while, even adults. As for Paul, I didn't like hearing what you said, but it's the truth. Our marriage was a bunch of crap," I said, using one of her terms.

"That really sucks."

"I've made a new life for myself, and now I'm hoping your mom does the same. Then the two of you will have something to look forward to."

"You think she will?"

"I don't know, but I hope she realizes her mistakes and makes some changes."

"Me, too."

"Me, too," I repeated, wondering whether Dana

wanted to change, whether she was ready to stop taking drugs and be a responsible parent.

"I lied earlier," Summer said, giving me a sidelong glance and an impish grin that reminded me of the child I'd known.

"About what?"

"Your pancakes don't suck. They rock."

I woke up early the next morning and discovered I'd fallen asleep on the floor, my arm around Summer, her head against my shoulder. My fingers tingled. I knew by my niece's slow even breathing that she was still asleep. Slowly, I pulled my arm free and grabbed a pillow off a nearby chair and wedged it under her head. Before leaving her bedroom, I covered her with a quilt.

I went into my bathroom and showered and while drying my hair, I thought I heard the phone ring. I opened the door and saw Summer coming down the stairs. "Would you get that, please?"

She picked up the receiver. "Hey, Mom!"

I took my robe from the back of the door, slipped it on and went to stand by my niece.

"Really? You mean it? Gee, that'll be awesome." Summer's face beamed with happiness. "I can't wait."

I motioned that I wanted to speak to Dana, but Summer shrugged and put the receiver back down. "Mom already hung up. She's out of the hospital. And she's coming for me this Saturday. Isn't that great?"

Part of me was relieved. I'd no longer shoulder the responsibility for my niece's care. Yet…the news left me anxious and more than a little worried about Dana caring for Summer. My sister and I would have a long talk. "Did she say how we can reach her?"

"No, only that she'd call Saturday to let us know when to expect her."

"Is Gram with her?"

Summer shrugged. "Beats me."

Uneasiness crawled up my spine, settled in my gut. "I'll call her apartment and talk to her," I said, taking the phone and punching in the numbers. A recording informed me the line was no longer in service.

"Your phone's been disconnected."

She shrugged. "Something gets cut off every couple of months."

"You mean this happens all the time?"

"Last month the power company shut off the electricity for almost a week. We pretended we were camping, and we ate tiny hot dogs straight out of the can. It was great fun until we ran out of candles. Then I had to sleep in the dark, and that was really creepy."

On Friday I called my supervisor to say I'd be back to work on Monday. I also arranged to meet my friends at DiMillo's for dessert, and Summer agreed to go with me.

Thankfully, she wore minimal white makeup. The

wide smile on her face made up for the heavily applied mascara and black lipstick. She'd spiked the hair on top of her head but left several soft wisps around her face. Summer had worn the black silk blouse I'd given her, unbuttoned at the neck with a hint of her pink T-shirt showing in the opened collar, giving her complexion a healthy glow.

When we arrived, the hostess led us to a table where Mallory and Carrie were waiting for us.

"Holy shit! This is some classy place," Summer said, covering her mouth and sending an apologetic look at my friends. "Oops, it just slipped out."

The waitress filled our glasses with water and handed us the menus.

Mallory laughed. "It's nothing we haven't heard before. And yes, this is a nice place."

Summer sat down, twisted around in her chair and stared out the window at a forty-foot yacht tied in its slip. "Wow, I bet that boat costs lots more than what my mom makes in a year."

"That boats costs more than all of us make in a year," Carrie said, smiling.

Mallory reached beneath the table and put a bright neon gift bag in front of Summer. "Annie said you liked black. It's one of my favorite colors, too. It brings out my naturally blond hair."

"Natural? Who are you kidding?" I asked.

Mallory winked at Summer who looked confused.

"They're jealous because I'm not afraid to help Mother Nature along."

Summer peeked in the bag and was about to put it down on the floor when Mallory reached in and pulled out a pair of lacy black stockings. "If you don't like these, I can exchange them for another pattern. Annie said you liked fishnets, but these are the latest, and I hear from my customers that these are the 'in thing.' But I do have fishnets at my shop if you'd prefer."

Summer looked down and slid her hand into the pantyhose and seemed to admire the delicate flower design. "No, these rock." A moment went by, then almost as an afterthought she said. "Thanks."

I sat back and relaxed. Tomorrow my life would get back to normal. And though I hated to see Summer leave with my sister, I also looked forward to living with Tony again. I missed him. I wasn't cut out to raise a troubled teenage girl.

Tomorrow my life would be simpler. Happier.

Meanwhile Summer would return to a mother who called her a bitch.

The waitress arrived with drinks.

Carrie said, "I took it upon myself to order for us. And Summer, since I didn't know what you like, I ordered my favorite, a Shirley Temple with a slice of orange and three cherries. I know it sounds girly, but they're so yummy. I got one for myself, too."

I expected Summer to complain.

She didn't reply right away and instead glanced down at her legs before looking up. "Oh, the drink is cool. I love cherries. Would it be all right if I went to the ladies' room and put on these stockings?"

"Sure, I'll go with you."

"Suit yourself."

When she exited the stall a while later, she lifted the long black skirt to show off her lace stockings. "Are these awesome or what?"

"They look pretty neat to me."

"I like your friends."

Our strained visit appeared to be headed for a nice ending.

We walked back to the table together.

"So how's your teenybopper?" Carrie asked Mallory.

I laughed. "Do you wave when he gets on the school bus?"

Mallory turned to Summer. "The man I'm dating is a few years younger, and these two are jealous. They wear makeup to cover up their green complexions."

Summer giggled, lifted her skirt and glanced at her stockings, then polished off her Shirley Temple. "Can I have one more?"

Mallory motioned to the waitress. "I've got this one." She also ordered thick slices of chocolate cake. "Those stockings do wonders for your legs," Mallory said, matter-of-factly. "You have such shapely calves, but then I'm sure you've heard that plenty."

Summer shook her head.

"That surprises me," Mallory continued. "It's my business to know about such things. Trust me, you've got the goods."

Summer's smile almost split her face in two as she extended her leg and looked down. "I can't wait to show these to my friends."

"And your fingers are long and feminine. If you want to show off your hands, you might consider putting tiny decals over your black nail polish. I have some with flowers and others with geometric shapes at my shop. If you're interested, you can drop over after we leave here." Mallory winked. "It never hurts for us girls to draw attention to our best assets."

Summer turned to me. "Can we?"

"Sure."

Summer gobbled up her chocolate cake and then polished off part of mine. She lifted her water goblet and examined it in the candlelight. "I see all kinds of colors. This is the prettiest glass I've ever drank from. I can't wait to tell my friends about this place."

Her voice rang with excitement. How little she'd experienced in life. I wanted to shelter her from my sister, to take Summer places and see her participate in sports. But that wasn't possible. She'd leave tomorrow, and I didn't know when I'd see her again. But I'd keep in touch, that's if they didn't move again. This time I'd give Summer a calling card and ask her to call me each week. And if she needed anything—a shoulder to cry on, books for school, advice, encouraging words—I'd make sure she got it.

"What kind of things do you do in L.A.?" Carrie asked.

"Stuff with friends, you know, the usual."

"Do you do sports?"

"Nah."

Carrie pulled out a picture from her wallet and handed it to Summer. "No one meets me and escapes without seeing at least one photo of my boys. They're adorable, don't you think?"

"Be careful what you say," Mallory said, tapping Summer's arm, "or you'll be hearing more than you ever wanted to know about the twins."

Carrie elbowed Mallory. "Don't pay any attention to her."

Summer's girlish giggle took me by surprise. *A very nice surprise.*

"They're cute. Too bad I'm going away because I'm a really good babysitter."

Mallory tipped her head back and laughed. "You don't know how lucky you are not to have to take care of those little hellions."

"Hey, watch what you say about my boys." Carrie smiled sheepishly. "But they can be a handful, and finding a sitter willing to put up with them more than once isn't easy."

"I bet I'd get along good with your boys. Little kids like me," Summer said with pride.

I knew so little about my niece.

"But I can't babysit because I'm leaving tomorrow. And the best part is Mom's renting a car, and we'll stop along the way home to see places. I can't wait. Maybe we'll even eat at a restaurant like this one."

How could Dana afford to travel cross-country when she couldn't pay her phone bill? For that matter how was she going to pay for her flight, unless Mom had bought the ticket?

I was relieved I wouldn't have to drop Summer off at the airport and watch her board a plane by herself.

At least now, I'd corner Dana, and we'd have a serious talk.

CHAPTER 8

Early the next morning I tried calling my sister's apartment and heard the same recording; her line had been disconnected. I also called my mom's house and left a message on her machine. Though I'd always considered myself to be a patient person, my patience had maxed out hours ago as I'd tossed and turned in bed, more questions than answers. Would Dana go along with my suggestion that Summer see a therapist? Would my sister stop taking drugs? In the past she'd assured me she'd only experimented but wasn't addicted. I knew better. Dana had a serious problem that needed more attention than the few days she'd gotten in the hospital.

I'd expected her to call either last night or this morning. If she was taking a flight into Portland, she needed to let me know when to pick her up at the airport. Frustration, anxiety and a strong feeling of dread pulsated through me.

"I'm glad you made pancakes for our last morning together. I'll sure miss these," Summer said, pushing a wedge of pancake into the syrup on her plate.

"We'll have lots more mornings together," I said, the lump in my throat thickening at the prospect of turning my niece over to Dana. "I plan for you to visit often. Maybe you can fly out after Christmas during your school vacation. And again during winter and spring break. I'm not losing track of my favorite niece again."

She giggled. "I'm your only niece."

"Well…even if I had a dozen other nieces, you'd still be my favorite.

"And these pancakes are easy to make. I'll give Dana a box of the mix and she can whip some up for you, too."

"My mom's not much of a cook, and she sometimes sleeps late, but I bet I could make some for myself. Maybe I'll make some for my mom, too."

She'd applied little makeup this morning and barely resembled the teenage girl I'd picked up at the airport, maybe because her sullen expression had vanished, maybe because her eyes twinkled with happiness. I hoped Dana didn't disappoint her.

"Anyway, I need to pack my stuff," Summer said, rising from the chair. "I kind of need a new bag for my things. Do you have one I can have?"

My insides clenched at the thought of her shoving her possessions into a trash bag. "Sure, help yourself."

"I still need to wash a few things, that's if there's time."

I glanced at the kitchen clock, saw it was already ten, then turned to the phone.

Ring, dammit, ring.

"We won't know how much time we have until Dana calls. But bring down what you want washed, and I'll get a load going."

"Mom said we'd rent a car, not just any car, but a sporty model with a ragtop so we can feel the wind through our hair as we cruise from state to state. She says we might take a month or six weeks. Can you imagine! Six weeks! We're going to have so much fun."

Typical Dana, not an ounce of common sense in her head. Harsh of me to think that way, but after years of watching my sister make bad, impulsive choices, I knew it was true. It was too cold in Maine to drive with the top down, and how would Dana rent any vehicle with her bad credit? Or afford to take an extended trip?

Ring, dammit, ring.

"What about school?"

"I hate school." She looked up. Our eyes locked for a moment. She shrugged. Something I couldn't decipher streaked across her face. "It's no big deal. Really. I can make it up later."

I was glad Vi wasn't around to hear that. We didn't need an argument to mar my niece's good mood.

"How are your grades?" I asked, thinking I could hire a tutor if she needed the help.

"I get by," she replied with a defensive look.

I picked up the plates and rinsed them. Summer surprised me by carrying the glasses and utensils to the sink. Our shoulders brushed, and I felt a close bond drawing us together.

"On the way to the airport, I thought we'd stop at the mall and pick up a duffel bag for you to pack your clothes in."

Looking offended, Summer paused a moment before speaking. "Mom warned me not to allow you or some other do-gooder to treat me like a charity case. I got plenty of clothes and everything I need."

Do-gooder.

It was as though a hundred fingernails had scraped a blackboard.

I was certain Summer hadn't meant to insult me, and I knew where the term originated.

Over the years my sister had accused me of being *Miss Goody Goody* to make her look bad.

"Consider it an early Christmas present. I'll ship your CD/DVD player and television next week."

I saw the surprise on her face. "You mean it?"

"I bought them for you."

"Is that cool or what!"

Tony came over for lunch. I grilled hamburgers and dished up chips and dill pickles.

Summer grabbed a plate and a can of Pepsi and darted a nervous glance at Tony. "I'm going to take this upstairs. I got lots more to do before my mom arrives."

"Have a nice trip," Tony said, sounding relieved he wouldn't have to exchange small talk with her.

She also seemed eager to leave the kitchen.

When we heard the soft click of her bedroom door closing, Tony stood and took me in his arms. Pent-up desire simmered between us.

"I've missed you," he murmured, kissing a path along the side of my face and nibbling on my right earlobe. "It's been one hell of a long week."

"Mmmmmm, you can say that again." I leaned into his chest, reveled in his warmth. I'd missed him. I'd missed his arm slung around my waist while I slept. I'd missed being awakened by his kisses.

"Have you heard from your sister?"

"Not yet, but she could call any minute." *And a big fat pig could grow wings and nest on top of my chimney.* "Dana is always losing track of time so I wouldn't be surprised to see her saunter in here late tonight or some time tomorrow."

Tony looked concerned. "You *are* expecting her to show, right?"

"Eventually."

"I sure hope it's soon because I need you."

Like I needed you this week.

Where had that come from?

Summer was my niece, my problem. I couldn't expect Tony to drop everything and hold my hand through every family crisis.

Or could I?

"In two days you move back in," I said, hoping to appease him. "By Monday evening, our lives will be back to normal."

By six I was concerned. By eight I'd begun to worry whether there had been an accident. But I'd listened to the news, and I'd even called the state police. It was a clear night, and all planes from L.A. were on schedule.

Unless she'd arrived on an earlier flight, or maybe she had decided to fly into Manchester, New Hampshire? Why hadn't Dana called?

I focused on the damn phone for the thousandth time that hour.

For supper I'd made grilled cheese sandwiches, but Summer had only taken one bite and pushed it away. For the past hour she'd sat on the couch staring blankly at the television screen, the voice muted, her shoulders hunched forward, her expression discouraged.

I couldn't just sit there so I alternated between walking into my room where I'd regroup and tell myself I was thinking the worst or pacing across the tile kitchen floor. Surely, Dana wouldn't let Summer down. She wouldn't do that to her daughter again. I was overreacting. Any minute that phone would ring or the door would swing open. Dana would smile and give me one of her many excuses.

"I've got a great idea, why don't we play a board game? I have Monopoly, Scrabble, checkers and others."

"Naah, I don't feel like it."

"Or we could bake some brownies for when your mom arrives."

She shook her head and stared at the television.

At eleven, we watched the news together. And when I wasn't ordering the phone to ring, I was cursing out Dana.

"Let's go to bed," I finally said at midnight.

Summer rose slowly, shook her head. "I don't understand what could have happened. She said she'd be here today. She promised."

I managed a smile, the muscles in my face aching from the effort. "I'm sure we'll hear from her tomorrow. She probably was flying standby and got bumped."

"Yeah, that must be it. She probably missed her flight. She's kinda late a lot."

I watched Summer walk up the stairs, looking as though it were an effort to lift one foot in front of the other.

Dana, where are you?

Ring, dammit, ring.

As if in a dream, I heard a bell and realized it was the phone. I blinked my eyes open, jumped out of bed and ran across the living room.

"Hello."

"Hey, Annie, it's Dana."

I glanced at the clock—3:00 a.m.

My stomach coiled. "Where have you been?"

"Don't get shook up. I couldn't call sooner."

I wanted to scream and rant, but no good would come of making a big fuss. "Summer's been waiting to hear from you all day."

"Well, something unexpected came up. Anyway, I called to tell you my news."

I hadn't realized I'd been holding my breath that I now blew out slowly. "Let me guess. You're already at the airport, waiting for us?"

"No, not even close."

"When are you flying in?"

"I'm not."

"A bus ride will save some money, but it's a long…"

"Do you think I'm stupid? No way in hell I'd take a bus clear across the country. I'm not coming to Maine."

"Damn."

"Take it easy. When I explain, you'll understand."

"All I understand right now is that you've disappointed Summer. You promised her this wonderful trip…"

"I'm going into rehab," Dana said.

"What happened between yesterday morning and today that changed your mind?"

"It turns out I don't have an apartment to go back to. When the cops showed up again, my landlady flipped out, packed up my things into two boxes and told me to never come back."

"She can't do that," I said, "without giving you a month's notice. You should check with legal aid."

"Well, I did, and it turns out I have no rights since the lease was in someone else's name, and they were behind in the rent."

"How could you allow this to happen?"

"I'm not perfect like you, that's why," she replied with that hateful tone I'd grown up with.

"Also the department of human services has threatened to take Summer away if I don't go into rehab. And if I lost Summer, I'll lose part of my welfare check. How am I supposed to get by if they cut my benefits?"

"Is that all Summer is to you, a larger welfare check?"

"I thought you'd be happy that I'm trying to turn my life around."

"That's not it, and you know it. You're always putting yourself ahead of Summer."

"Yeah, well… I'm not perfect like you. Besides, I can use the break and some away time from that kid."

"Are you referring to your daughter?"

"Sure, who else?"

"She's just a young girl who needs her mother's love and attention."

"She's a pain in the ass kid with a fresh mouth. I don't know how I've put up with her all these years."

Anger coursed through my bloodstream. "You disgust me."

"What else is new? Anyway, Mom says she'll have Summer's school records forwarded to you, so will you take the kid?"

"For how long?"

"Six weeks."

Summer would be separated from her friends. And she clearly had good friends at home because she talked about how she couldn't wait to share her adventures with them. Summer would have to start at a new school at the worst possible time for a child. Thirteen was the most awkward, tough age in a teen's life. And, there was Tony. Six weeks was a long time to put our relationship on hold.

"Anyway, if you turn me down, she's going into foster care."

"I won't allow you to dump Summer on a stranger's doorstep," I said, my voice shaking with rage. "I'll take her."

"I knew you were too much of a do-gooder to turn me down."

"You'd better get your act together."

"Aye, aye, sir."

As angry as I was with Dana, I realized Summer staying with me would be good for my niece. She'd finally get the love and attention she deserved. She'd see a therapist. When she returned home with her mother, she'd have a new wardrobe, and I hoped, a new outlook on life. "Work hard in rehab. Don't disappoint Summer again."

"This isn't about the kid, it's about me."

"You're a selfish bitch."

CHAPTER 9

The line went dead. How dare Dana hang up on me? I slammed down the receiver and turned. In the glow from the night-light I kept plugged in the living room, I saw Summer standing near the stairway.

My heart stilled for a moment, then beat double time. How much had she heard?

"Mom's not coming for me, is she?" Her tone sounded hollow, like someone who'd given up on life.

"No, she's not, but in a way it's good news. She's going back into drug rehab, and when she's released, she'll be better equipped to manage her life and care for you."

"That sounds like a bunch of crap."

More empty promises.

This child had been disappointed too many times. I wanted to make it up to her but didn't know how.

She exhaled a wobbly breath. "For how long?"

"Six weeks." Wanting to take her in my arms as I had the other night, I moved forward.

Summer backed up onto the first step.

The close bond we'd shared earlier crumbled.

"Try to look on the bright side. We'll have six more weeks together. And think of all the fun we can have. I'll even teach you how to cook some of your favorite foods."

In the dim light I saw tears trailing down her face. "I don't care whether she ever comes back."

"You have the right to be angry. After you've had a chance to think about it, I hope you'll see that this is for the best for both you and your mother. Once you've started school and made new friends, you'll feel more comfortable here."

She folded her arms across her chest. "I'm not going to any hick school. I'll make up the work when I get back to L.A."

"Six weeks is too much time to make up. Besides, you have to go to school. It's the law. Maybe you can try out for a team or take part in after school activities."

Maybe six weeks together would undo some of the damage Dana had done.

I stepped forward.

She sniffed and backed up another step.

"We don't have a choice. This is something Dana has to do, for herself and for you."

She backed up two more steps, stood staring down at me. "You're such a fake. I heard the conversation. She dumped me here, and now you're stuck with me. You don't want me either."

"Of course I want you...."

"Like hell you do."

"Summer, let's talk about this."

She turned, scrambled up the stairs. When she reached the top, she glanced over her shoulder. "I hate her."

"You don't mean that," I said, at a loss for what to say.

Early the next morning, I tiptoed into Summer's bedroom. She was curled up on her side, her face tearstreaked. I saw the stockings Mallory had given her on the floor by the bed, shredded. I remembered her pride when she'd admired her legs clad in those same stockings.

Ruined, beyond repair.

Was Summer's life beyond repair?

As I neared, I saw a nail file sticking through the body of Vi's small moose, now headless and destroyed.

Another casualty.

My heart went out to Summer, and I wanted to rock her in my arms. But I doubted she'd let me touch her. Whatever progress we'd made had disintegrated with Dana's phone call.

Depressed, I went back downstairs. Not knowing where else to turn, I called Tony. "I need you. Please come right over."

"Babe, what's wrong?"

"Dana is going into a treatment program."

Tony cursed. "How long will Summer be with you this time?"

"Six weeks."

More cursing, followed by an exasperated groan. "Let me guess. Your family expects you to bear the brunt of this. It's not fair. Someone else should be willing to take that kid for a while."

The way he'd said *that kid* offended me.

"She's my niece, and I love her."

"Your family's taking advantage of you. You're too meek to say no to them."

Anger knotted my stomach. "Damn you, I'm not some mild-mannered fool who's too weak to stand up for herself. This is about family and sticking together. Who else is going to take care of Summer if I don't?"

A moment of silence. "Sorry, I know you love the kid, and you're her aunt and want to be there for her. You're kind and generous, which is one of the things I love most about you. Give me a few minutes to shower and get dressed. I'll be there with donuts and coffee."

"Thanks."

After I hung up, the phone rang. "Make mine a Boston Crème," I said, thinking Tony had called back.

"Annie, it's Mom."

"Where have you been? I've left messages on your machine."

"Hank surprised me by showing up three days ago so no one's home to listen to the messages. I've been trying to talk some sense into Dana who checked herself out of the hospital against the doctor's advice. Then I went with her to her apartment. What a rat-infested nest that was. She no longer has a place to stay."

"She told me."

"What she probably didn't tell you is that her wonderful friends bailed on her and left her holding the bag. Dana's been charged with possession. I had to hire an attorney who persuaded a judge to drop the charges if she agreed to go into rehab. Which is her only hope. If she doesn't stay straight, this time she's going to jail."

"Poor Summer."

"Yes, that child has been through a lot. I wish I could take her in, but our condo association is very strict about children staying for more than a week. I could take her for several days, but no longer."

"I don't want her tossed back and forth from one person to the other." Though a week-long break would have been nice. But I couldn't do that to my niece. To Summer this would be more proof that I didn't want her.

"Have you spoken to the school about sending her grades?"

"No, I figured I'd talk to you first and make sure you can keep her for the next month and a half. If so, I'll take care of everything tomorrow morning."

"Yes, I'll take Summer while Dana is in rehab, but Dana had better work hard because I'm sick of hearing her excuses."

And I have a life, too. With Tony. I'd ask him to move back in right away. It wasn't fair to us to stay apart for six long weeks. And I'd need his emotional support if I was going to get through this in one piece.

"Dana understands how important it is for her to stay sober and away from drugs. She almost died. That should jolt some sense into her."

"I sure hope so."

"Take care, sweetie. I'll get back to you soon."

When I heard Tony's key in the lock, I went to greet him. He placed the box of donuts and a bag on the table and opened his arms. I walked into his embrace and savored the feel of him, inhaled his scent. "I don't want us to be apart any longer. Move back in tonight."

He trailed kisses along my face. His lips settled firmly over mine, taking away my breath. "I've missed you."

"Same here."

"Babe, you look beat."

"After Dana called, I couldn't sleep."

"Go sit down on the couch, and I'll bring in our coffee and donuts. I got you a Boston Crème."

He'd remembered. "You're so thoughtful."

"I aim to please," he said, his mouth curving into a crooked grin.

I opened the cupboard and reached for the plates, but he shooed me away. "I'm taking care of everything, so go sit down and allow me to wait on you."

I did as I was told. Immense relief washed over me. It felt so good not to be alone to face my problems. I loved Summer, but six weeks was a long time to deal with her. I longed for a strong shoulder to rest my head on, someone to talk to and help me decide what was best for my niece.

Tony arrived a moment later with our donuts and coffee. He sat next to me and put the cardboard cup into my hands. "I want you to relax. I'm here for you. Just tell me what you want me to do."

"Don't leave."

"I'm not going anywhere."

We sat munching our donuts and sipping coffee, shoulder to shoulder, hip to hip. His nearness comforted me as did the companionable silence between us.

I heard a noise and turned, watched Summer stomp down the stairs, her heavy black boots unlaced, her face masked in white. Thick black lines zigzagged down her cheeks.

I turned to Tony and saw fleeting disgust in his eyes that disappeared the instant he smiled. "There are donuts and juice in the kitchen."

She marched by, her expression defiant.

Tony's jaw tightened. "Your aunt deserves a civil reply."

"Bite me," she said, her face contorting into a mean sneer.

"Summer, that's not…" I said.

She continued into the kitchen and banged the door, returned a moment later with a donut and a paper cup. Head hanging low, she passed by us without a word. I was relieved since I feared she'd throw out another insult.

Once she'd slammed the bedroom door, I sighed and moved closer to Tony.

"You're going to allow her to speak to me that way?"

"Of course not. I tried to correct her, but I couldn't very well shout while she was in the kitchen, and by the time she came out, I thought it might be better not to say anything. She needs time to get over her disappointment."

"She needs to know you're the boss. She needs to be cut down a notch or two and made to realize there are rules, and she needs to follow them. Or she'll find herself with nowhere to go."

She's only thirteen. "I'd never throw her out. She has enough to worry about and already feels that she's a burden no one wants."

"She is a burden, and it's no wonder with that raunchy attitude." He shook his head, looked as though he didn't understand me. We'd always been able to talk about anything. Until now, we'd been on the same wavelength.

But no more.

"You've got your hands full, but I can't help you," he said.

"What are you saying?"

"I won't live in this house while she's here. She'd drive me crazy."

"I thought I could count on you."

"You can. I'll come over occasionally. We'll spend some evenings together. I'll eat supper here. But at night, I'll need a place to unwind."

"You can unwind here, with me," I said, hoping to change his mind.

Spend the nights holding me in our bed, loving me.

"I'm sorry, and I feel like a jackass for letting you down. But I can't move in. You saw how Summer looked at me. I won't take that insolent behavior from any child. If I stay here, I'll say something to her that I'll regret. This could tear us apart."

"Not if we don't let it."

"I love you. I want to be with you, but trust me on this. My moving in will only complicate the issue. Summer doesn't want me near, and if you hope to get through to her and have some peace, I can't live here."

His reasoning sounded valid. And he almost had me convinced he had Summer's best interests in mind.

Almost, but not quite.

"Aren't you getting tired of staying in a motel?"

"Yes. I've already talked to my tenant who wants me to stay there and split expenses."

"You had this figured out before you came here," I said, shaking my head in disgust.

"Don't make it sound like I don't want to be with you. Because I do. But I cannot tolerate being in the same room with your niece. You want the truth, there it is. And don't make me out to be some monster. When we decided to live together, I made it clear, I didn't want any kids. I'd meant our own, but I certainly don't want to live with one who speaks to me the way she does."

Frustration welled inside, made me want to beat my fists against his chest, made me want to scream and cry. Tony disappointed me, but I'd seen that hateful look on Summer's face. I couldn't blame him for wanting to escape.

Especially when he didn't want to be around children.

And Summer wasn't just any child. She came with more baggage than most.

Was I upset he wasn't moving in?

You bet.

But as disappointed as his declaration made me, I saw his point.

That didn't change facts. Tony had chosen the easy way out.

Just like Dana's friends, who'd abandoned her, Tony was bailing out.

CHAPTER 10

On Monday Vi volunteered to watch Summer so I could return to work. I was glad to escape yet concerned about my former mother-in-law's determination to turn Summer's life around. I appreciated Vi's help, but I'd warned her to proceed with caution. She scoffed and reminded me of her years teaching seventh- and eighth-grade children. Though she certainly knew a lot more than I did, I worried that her expectations for Summer might be too high.

I stood in my niece's bedroom and pleaded with her to unlock the door. "Summer, please come out of the bathroom."

"Not until that old witch leaves."

"I won't have you talking that way about Vi."

"Then tell her to split."

"I can't do that."

"I don't need a sitter. I've taken care of myself plenty of times."

"I'll feel better knowing you aren't here alone. And Vi is looking forward to spending the day with you."

"That's crap, and you know it."

"I'm already late, so I have to leave. I hope you'll try to get along with Vi. I know you're disappointed about having to stay with me for six more weeks, but once you've had a chance to calm down, I hope you'll realize how important it is for your mom to be in rehab. Make the best of this situation. I'll talk to you later when I get home from work."

From the other side of the door—silence.

Vi assured me she could handle the situation.

I could not.

Once I'd escaped to my garage, I cried. But there wasn't time to fall apart so I dried my eyes, stuck the key into the ignition and backed out of my driveway.

When I threw my purse on top of the filing cabinet thirty minutes later, I was already exhausted.

My administrative assistant, Roberta, knocked on the door and walked into my office. "Good morning, Annie. Would you like me to get you a cup of coffee? You look like you could use one."

I shuffled through the pile of memos on my desk. "Yes, thanks, you're a lifesaver. Do I have any appointments or messages for today?"

"Yes, the LePages are closing on their loan at four. Anita from Hayes and Dalton called to say they've completed the title search for River View Estates."

I jotted a note. "Please call Anita back and ask her to check on the Philbrook account. Is there anything else?"

"Yes, Ms. Wilcox is gunning for you. She's been here to look for you three times in the last hour."

My supervisor, Edith Wilcox, in her mid-forties, rarely smiled and insisted on total dedication from her staff. Her piercing gray eyes and tall stature gave her a commanding presence that dared anyone to disagree. According to Edith, she'd never married because her career came first. I admired her dedication.

After Paul's death, I'd thrown myself into my work, arriving early and leaving late. I'd even worked some weekends. My efforts were noticed, and I quickly rose through the ranks, due partially to Edith's recommendations.

I glanced at my watch. "I'm only thirty minutes late."

"Late is late. Thirty minutes or thirty seconds. It's all the same to Ms. Wilcox." We heard the click of heels and Roberta stepped back to look into her office. "Here's the general now. Good luck," she said, making a quick getaway.

Edith marched across the room and stopped inches from my desk. "I trust you've taken care of your family emergency and are now prepared to work."

If Edith were a flower, she'd be prickly cactus that bloomed once each year, a no-nonsense-keep-your-distance plant.

The intercom on my desk buzzed. "It's Mrs. Violet Jacobs. Do you want me to tell her you'll call her back?"

My heartbeat shifted into high gear.

Damn, what was wrong now?

"No, I'll take it," I said, biting down on my lower lip and grabbing the phone.

"I wanted you to know that Summer came out of her room long enough to grab an English muffin and juice. She'll be fine, and I'll manage, so please try not to worry about us."

"That's a tall order, but I'll certainly try."

"Would you mind if I tried to find a therapist for Summer? I'd like to get her some help as soon as possible."

I looked at Edith, disapproval darkening her brown eyes.

"We'll talk about this when I get home. Maybe Summer's school will recommend someone."

"All right but I want to move quickly on this. I know what I'm talking about."

"I'm sure you do. Thanks for everything."

"It's nothing."

Edith cleared her throat and leafed through a stack of files on my desk.

"I have to go. Good luck."

"I don't need luck because I have experience on my side."

I hope you're right. "Bye."

I put the phone down. "Sorry for the interruption. My niece will be staying with me for six more weeks. Once she's enrolled in school, it'll be simpler," I said.

"That's what you think. My younger sister is forever running to school to pick up a sick child or to speak with a teacher." She shook her head and smiled at me. "That's precisely why I never had children. I didn't want to clutter my life." She pulled a chair next to my desk. "I want to go over these reports with you. I thought we'd grab a quick bite for lunch in the deli next door and order out for supper. That's if you can work late."

"That's kind of tough for me right now, with my niece here and all. She needs a lot of attention."

Displeasure darkened Edith's gray eyes.

"But I'm sure I can find someone to watch her so I can stay later," I said, hoping Vi was free.

"That's good because we have a lot of catching up to do. Also I got word from the powers that Blanche will be out on maternity leave, and they'd like you to take up the slack."

Which meant more overtime.

Edith's lips curved into a wide smile. "Of course, you'll get a nice bonus at the end of December."

Uneasiness crept up my spine.

I couldn't expect Vi to devote her life to my niece. Summer was my responsibility. She'd need transportation to school activities and doctors' appointments. And even if Vi were willing to stay with Summer 24/7, I wanted to be a part of my niece's life.

But I didn't want to lose my job.

Or Tony. He was never far from my thoughts. Though lately I found myself doubting his dedication to me.

He'd called last night to say he was sorry about how things went, but he hoped I understood how he felt. And he couldn't wait to see me again.

Roberta buzzed me. "Ms. Turgeon, the principal at The Gray, New Gloucester Middle School is on line three."

I cast a tentative glance at Edith, who drummed her fingers against my desk. I considered telling Roberta to take a message, but I knew Edith would be here for a while. And if I didn't take care of this first, I'd have trouble focusing. "Put her through." I placed my hand over the receiver. "This'll only take a minute."

She waved me along. "Sure, sure. Just get on with it."

"Is this Ms. Annie Jacobs?"

"Yes, it is."

"I've received your niece's transcripts along with documentation declaring you Summer's temporary guardian. It's imperative we get together soon to discuss her curriculum."

"Can I meet with you early some morning this week?"

"Normally that would be fine, but I'm teaching a seminar this week. If you're available, I can see you at two this afternoon. Otherwise, this'll have to wait until Friday. But I'd hoped to get Summer into a program right away."

I looked into Edith's face. A small vein in her temple pulsed, the tension between us palpable. But I couldn't abandon Summer.

"Ms. Jacobs, are you still there?"

"Yes, I was checking my schedule. I'll be there at two."

"I'll see you then."

I hung up the phone and looked at Edith, her expression sober and intense.

When I turned into the driveway that evening, it was already 8:30. Vi greeted me at the door. "You look beat."

I walked inside and hung my coat in the hall closet. "It's been a long day. How's Summer?"

"She spent most of the time in her bedroom. I went up there to try to make conversation, but she ignored me."

"I'm sorry to hear that."

"I must admit I'm a bit disappointed. Since I don't have any grandchildren, I'd hoped your niece would want to be my adopted granddaughter. But that's not going to happen."

"Maybe in time it will."

Vi put on her coat and hat, and I walked her to the door.

"How did it go at the school?" Vi asked.

"The principal is concerned about Summer's low test scores and her poor attendance record. And according to her teachers back in L.A., Summer exhibits lack of motivation, no respect for authority and is possibly developmentally challenged."

"I'd hate to see that child lost in the system among problem children."

"This is just temporary until she returns to L.A." I didn't like to think of Summer struggling to keep up with her classmates. "Will you be able to watch Summer tomorrow while I work?"

Vi hesitated. "I don't have anything planned during the day, but my evenings for the rest of the week are booked. Tomorrow I'm the speaker at the Women's Literary Union meeting. They asked me months ago, and I told them I'd be there. I don't see how I can cancel on such short notice."

"I don't expect you to change your schedule. I'll be home early tomorrow. No problem."

The knot in my stomach tightened.

My responsibilities at work conflicted with my other obligations. As much as I dreaded asking for more time off, I wouldn't have a choice unless I found someone to help with Summer.

Vi ticked off on her fingers. "This Wednesday it's my turn to host my reading group, and I usually bowl on Thursdays but I could skip that for a week if you need me."

"I won't hear of it," I said, sounding calm, though I wasn't. "Summer starts school this Wednesday. I appreciate you being here with her tomorrow. I'll figure something out for the rest of the week."

"If you need to start work earlier in the morning, I wouldn't mind coming here each day to see that Summer gets on the bus safely."

Summer wouldn't appreciate having Vi watch out for her. She was old enough to get on the bus herself, but I wasn't willing to take any chances. If I wasn't able to be there, I'd take Vi up on her offer.

"Thanks, I'll keep that in mind."

On Tuesday, I left work early. Edith looked upset, but I had no choice. And when I got home, Vi was happy to be released of her duties, which made me wonder whether her day had gone worse than she'd said. I offered to take Summer shopping for school clothes. After stopping for burgers and fries, Summer asked if I'd stop at the Goodwill store, where she chose another pair of black combat boots, but these were her size. Either they looked better than the other pair or I'd grown accustomed to her choice of footwear. We also stopped by Mallory's shop and my friend insisted on giving Summer another pair of stockings and decals for her nails.

Wednesday morning I'd expected Summer to fuss about going to school. She said nothing. I cooked pancakes for breakfast, but she only ate two bites and pushed her plate away.

Fortunately, she wore minimal white makeup and a yellow top I'd bought her under a new black shirt Mallory insisted had been wasting away in her shop. I was thankful for my friend's help.

When the bus arrived shortly after seven, I waved to Summer who climbed the steps, her expression defiant and sullen.

Work was hectic and as the day wore on, I realized I'd have to stay late. But I couldn't leave Summer alone at home. I couldn't ask Vi to cancel her plans. And if I didn't prove I could handle my position at the bank, I could possibly be demoted. Not that I'd heard of anyone losing a promotion, but if I couldn't do the work, they'd find someone who could.

I saw no solution. Until Carrie called.

"Annie, if you aren't busy for supper, I was hoping you and Summer would join the boys and me. I'm making a salad and a large pan of lasagna."

"I'd love to, but I have to work late."

"Then maybe Summer would like to come over. I could pick her up after school, and you could join us later."

"You don't mind?"

"No problem, she can entertain my boys while I cook."

"Are you sure about this? You aren't afraid of her being a bad example?"

Her reassuring laugh gave me hope. "Have you considered that my hellions might be a bad influence on her? Just call the school and tell them I'll be picking her up. I don't mind, really. And plan on eating when you get here."

"It could be late?"

"And you'll be hungry. We can catch up on what's happening."

"Thanks, I owe you."

"Maybe I'll let you take my boys some weekend."

My moan was greeted by more laughter.

I was blessed with great friends.

Later that evening, I sat at Carrie's kitchen table, sipping a cup of coffee.

"Summer's really good with my boys. Normally they're so wound after school they drive me nuts. Having her here to entertain them gave me a break. So if you need a place for her to stay after school, it's no problem. It'd help me out," Carrie said, dishing up a large serving of lasagna.

"Are you sure?"

"As a matter of fact I was thinking of paying her while she's here. I figure she can use the money, and I can use the help. I was hoping the responsibility might help boost her self-esteem."

"I should be paying you."

"Don't be ridiculous. You have no idea how great it was having her around."

"Thanks, I appreciate all you're doing." My tense muscles relaxed, and I let out a sigh.

Everything would work out fine.

CHAPTER 11

When I got home that night, Summer seemed like a different child, her voice animated, her smile wide, her eyes sparkling with excitement.

"Ms. Carrier, my gym teacher, rocks. She wants me to try out for the basketball team. The school will provide the uniform, but I'll need to get a pair of shoes and a physical. Even when I explained I'd only be in Maine a little while, she said I could still play."

Summer thrust a piece of paper at me. "There's an activity fee, but Carrie said she wants me to work for her taking care of her boys. I'll pay you back, but I need the money now."

She cast a tentative glance at me and bit down on her lower lip. For a moment I saw myself in her. We had similar shaped eyes, the same bad habit.

I read the paper. The activity fee was fifty bucks, and a doctor was doing physicals at the school for ten dollars. "I can swing the money so don't worry about that."

"Mean it?"

"Definitely."

"You rock."

I rock!

It didn't get any better than this.

The next morning I prepared breakfast as usual. Summer cleaned her plate and asked for seconds. She again wore a black skirt, a black blouse unbuttoned to her waist with a bright green T-shirt underneath. She'd brushed her hair into soft curls, and her black fingernails were decorated with the decals Mallory had given her.

"How'd school go yesterday?"

"Okay."

"Did you get your homework done?"

"Most of it."

"Are you having trouble with something?"

"It's no big deal."

"If there's something you don't understand, just ask."

"It's not a big deal. Really. Did you sign the permission slip so I can try out for the team?"

"Yes, and I've called Carrie who'll take you shopping for shoes this afternoon, then drop you back off at the school for tryouts. I wrote out a check so you should be all set. I hope to go watch the practice."

"You don't have to."

"I want to."

A slight smile quirked the corner of her mouth.

Edith would be upset.

But Summer would be here for a few short weeks, and I'd be there for her. If necessary, I'd take work home to do over the weekend.

"Carrie says she'll bring Eric and Derrick for a little while to watch me play, until they start to dismantle the gym." Summer giggled. "Carrie gripes a lot about her kids, but I don't think she means any of it."

"She'd do anything for her sons," I said, thinking of all the sacrifices she'd made over the years. "She's a good friend and an even better mom."

For a moment a distant look claimed Summer's face. *Was she comparing her mother to Carrie?*

I worked through lunch so I could leave early and managed to arrive a few minutes before basketball practice started. The coach had divided the team into two groups, the blue shirts and the white shirts.

I spotted Summer right away; her black hair with the red stripe was hard to miss. She wore blue gym shorts and a blue shirt. I sat beside Carrie on the bleachers and watched my niece score a basket.

I jumped up and cheered. "Way to go, Summer. Do it again."

Looking pleased but embarrassed, she lowered her head and ran to the other end of the basketball court.

"Thanks for taking her shopping," I said to Carrie who had a hold of Eric's arm and was threatening bodily harm. Derrick was jumping from one bleacher to the other, but since there weren't any other parents near us, he wasn't bothering anyone.

Carrie brushed a strand of hair from her forehead and handed the boys cookies and juice boxes. "Summer has a calming effect on my twins. It's a pleasure to go shopping with her because she holds their hands, and for some strange reason, they listen to her. While at the shoe store, the boys settled down and they tried on winter boots. We also ran in to Wal-Mart, and not once did I have to raise my voice." She angled a warning glance at the boys. "If you two don't sit down this instant, I'm leaving right now."

The children hopped down onto the seat in front of us and stayed there for about three seconds.

"How's Tony taking all this?" Carrie asked, indicating Summer who'd just scored another basket.

"I've barely seen him. He blames my work schedule, but I know better," I said, tired of his lame excuses.

"Children can wreak havoc with a relationship. I should know. Whenever I have more than one date with a nice guy and he begins to look at me as though he cares a little, I introduce him to my boys." She snapped her fingers together. "Just like that, he's gone. In your case it's only temporary. Summer will only be here another five weeks."

I loved my niece, and I'd even gotten accustomed to the red stripe in her hair. I leaped up and waved my arms as Summer scored another two points. "Woo-hoo!"

A moment later, the score was tied. My niece stood on the foul line ready to shoot.

The boys leaned in close to me. "What's Summer doing?"

"She's going to shoot for the basket." I crossed my fingers and held my breath.

The boys mimicked me.

Carrie chuckled. "It's only a practice game. I'd hate to see the three of you at the real thing."

Summer aimed.

Whoosh.

I shouted until my voice grew hoarse.

The next week Dana called to say she'd sworn off drugs for good. She talked on the phone with Summer for almost an hour. I overheard my niece telling her mother about the basketball team and how she'd scored the winning point at practice. I also heard her discussing the trip they'd take once Dana was released.

I needed to have a talk with Summer about keeping her expectations in line about what her mother could and could not do.

Tony spent the next evening watching television with us. Summer had assured me she wouldn't lash out. She mainly ignored him but managed to grunt out a reply the few times he spoke to her. I'd been relieved when she went up to her room around eight.

Before Tony left, he promised to return Friday night

to cook supper for my niece and me—spaghetti and meatballs, my favorite. After a long good-night kiss that curled my toes, I stood at the door and waved as he backed his Porsche out of my driveway.

I counted my blessings: my sister in rehab. My niece had finally agreed to speak to the school therapist. And with a little nurturing, my love life would survive our short hiatus.

On Thursday, I received a call from the principal asking me to meet her before work on Friday morning. I drove Summer to school and tried to reassure her.

"You worry too much." But inside apprehension stirred, left me feeling queasy.

"This really sucks," Summer said, frowning.

"Don't assume this is a bad thing."

"Yeah, right. Like teachers and especially principals ever do anything but bitch."

I could tell she spoke from experience. "I thought we'd agreed you weren't using that language anymore."

"I'm right you know. Ms. Turgeon's gonna tell you a bunch of crap, and you'll get mad at me."

"No matter what anyone says, I won't be angry with you. If you're having some trouble with your school-work, then we'll do something about it before it's too late. Do you know what this meeting's about?"

"Beats me." Summer shrugged and climbed out of my Volvo, her head bent, shoulders sagging. I watched her saunter across the parking lot and stand by herself near the entry.

I hurried into the building and walked into the office. Several students were hanging around the secretary's desk. One had forgotten her lunch money, another needed to use the phone to call home because he felt sick and one child was crying and holding a bloody paper towel over her knee.

The secretary ushered the injured child into the nurse's office and returned, and even though the day had just begun, she looked exhausted.

I gave her my name.

"Ms. Turgeon is expecting you. Go right in."

The principal was on the phone so she gestured for me to sit down. A few seconds later she hung up and instructed the secretary not to interrupt us.

"Can I get you a cup of coffee?" she asked, shutting the door to her office.

"No, I'm all set. Is there a problem with Summer?"

"There's no easy way to say this." Ms. Turgeon cupped her hands together and paused.

My heart dropped.

"According to Summer's teachers, she's disruptive, won't follow directions and hasn't turned in a completed assignment since she arrived."

"I spoke to her gym teacher the other night at practice—"

"Gym's the only subject your niece is passing."

I leaned back in the chair to catch the breath knocked out of me. I hadn't expected straight A's, but... "What can I do?"

Ms. Turgeon shuffled through some papers in a folder. "Summer's standardized tests scores came back. She's way below grade level in every subject. Either she has a severe learning disability..."

I braced myself, chewed on my lower lip, and didn't give a damn if I looked unsure of myself. I was not confident and didn't care who knew.

"...or she's lazy and refusing to do the work."

"Summer isn't lazy," I said.

"The alternative could be worse."

"What do we do?"

"She'll need to take some additional standardized tests, and depending on the outcome, she may have to work with a special ed. teacher. Unfortunately by the time the test results are in, Summer's stay in Maine will be ending. And since she's here for just a few weeks, we can't expect much progress. Her teachers think Summer would do better in a lower grade."

"You mean demote her? She'd be crushed. Summer's very bright." Or had been at age eight.

"I hope so, but don't expect too much from her."

I'd help her with her schoolwork and ask Vi to tutor Summer. *Ms. Turgeon was wrong. The teachers were wrong. Those test scores were wrong. Summer was a smart child.*

What proof did I have?

The traitorous thought slammed into me.

The principal handed me an orange sheet of paper. "Meanwhile, are you aware of our policy for extracurricular activities?"

"No."

The paper explained the fees and the rules for each player. I scanned each line and found the kicker near the bottom of the page. No child will be allowed to participate in any sport or after school activity if that student flunks more than one subject.

"Are you saying Summer won't be allowed to play basketball?"

"I'm sorry, but it's the policy."

"Summer has blossomed since she started playing basketball. Surely, you can make an exception in this case."

Once more she shook her head. "That wouldn't be fair to the other pupils."

"I'm not sure you understand the kind of life Summer has endured. It'd be a shame to deny her something she truly enjoys and that's making such a positive impact on her life. Please, don't take that away from her."

"I don't have a choice. Summer needs to understand that good grades are important. If she refuses to work, then she has herself to blame."

I could tell by the firm set of her jaw that nothing I could say would change her mind. I understood the school couldn't function without rules, and that Summer had to live within guidelines.

But I feared this latest news would undo the progress she'd made.

"That really blows," Summer said, tears rimming her eyes, when I spoke to her shortly before Tony was due to arrive.

"We'll work together and get your ranks up."

"I only have four weeks left. No way in hell I'll be able to bring my grades up in time to be on the team."

"There'll be other teams when you go back to L.A. If you study hard now, you can join them."

She pursed her mouth. "This sucks. I knew the meeting would be bad news. I told you, didn't I?"

Her frustration seemed directed at me. "What did you expect? You weren't completing any of your assignments. If you want to play on the team, you need to earn that right. You need to work hard and earn passing ranks."

"I can't do that."

"Why not?"

"'Cause I'm stupid, that's why," she said, certainty and pain ringing in her tone. She turned and ran, slamming the kitchen door behind her.

CHAPTER 12

As Tony stirred the homemade spaghetti sauce, my mouth watered. The smell of oregano and thyme permeated the room.

"Summer needs to learn to follow rules," he said. "I know you don't want to hear this, but that kid is nothing but trouble. Mark my work, if Summer doesn't change her ways, she'll end up doing time in jail."

"You certainly don't sound particularly sympathetic."

"I know she's had a tough life, but she needs to shape up. Of course I'm sorry about her situation."

"You could fool me."

"I can understand how she must be feeling, but she has herself to blame. She needs to respect authority. Until she settles down and does what's asked of her, she'll continue to lose out."

"This really fries me. I don't blame Summer for staying in her room and refusing to eat with us. She can sense your animosity."

This wasn't fair to Tony, but I was way beyond being fair. I'd tried to reason with the principal, but I'd left her office knowing they could not change policy for one child. Otherwise, it wouldn't be fair to the other children. No one focused on what was fair for Summer. But I hadn't given up yet. I intended to check out the teen basketball program at the YMCA. If that panned out, maybe Summer could play on their team. Maybe I'd use that as leverage to make her study.

"Playing basketball was so important to her," I said, sighing.

"I know it's important, but…"

I raised my hand. "Let me guess. It's more important for her to learn to get along in school and to follow the rules."

"Precisely. You wanted the truth, and it's how I feel. For your sake, I hope I'm wrong."

Until now, I hadn't seen this side of Tony. Cold and uncaring. Did I want to be with someone like this? I wasn't in the right state of mind to make decisions about my future, but the question remained on the fringes of my mind.

He poured the pasta into a large bowl and sat next to me. "I love you, but you're setting yourself up for a big disappointment. You need to face facts. Your niece isn't about to change overnight, and she may never change. You can't fix thirteen years of neglect in six weeks."

"I know that."

"Do you? You sure don't act as though you do."

"I just want her to have a good time while she's here. Taking away the one thing that's important to her isn't a positive step. I understand she needs to know there are consequences to her actions, but in this case, the person responsible for Summer's low grades is Dana. Summer's a great kid, and given a little time, she'll bring her ranks up and prove to you and everyone in that school that she's a bright child," I said, my voice brittle. "And she'll grow to become a successful adult."

"If you had more time, you'd turn her life around. A few weeks won't do it, and what's going to happen when she returns home with your sister?"

That worried me. "I'll follow up on her progress even after she leaves." But from this distance, I could do little about Summer's education. I couldn't force Dana to keep Summer in therapy.

"Babe, I've been looking forward to spending tonight with you. I didn't want to depress you. Let's declare a truce. Let me take you and Summer to the movies tomorrow night…as a peace offering to try to cheer you both up."

"Aren't you afraid Summer might be a bad influence on you?"

His forehead furrowed. "Please don't allow this to come between us."

"You're the one letting this come between us." But if I didn't calm down and get control of my emotions, I could permanently sever the ties with the man I loved.

"I'm doing my best," he said with enough sincerity to appease me.

Was his best good enough?

What a crummy thought, and so unfair to Tony. Summer wasn't his responsibility. Was I now making excuses for him?

"I know."

"Good, then let's eat. And if you can persuade Summer to stop winging insults at me, I'll do my damnedest to get along with her."

"Summer assured me she'd never do that again."

His mouth lifted in a lopsided grin. "I'm relieved to hear that."

"Also, after Summer leaves, Vi wants us to have supper at her house."

He winked. "That 'old bag' probably intends to grill me instead of the steak."

"Don't call Vi that." The obvious insult was more than I could bear.

"Hey, you know I was kidding. In the past you've laughed."

"True, but…a lot's happened since then, and it's not funny anymore.

"I miss the way you were, the way we were—carefree and happy."

Would we ever be that way again?

He grabbed my hand and kissed my fingertips. "Am

I forgiven? I didn't mean to insult Vi. I'd think more of her, if she liked me."

This was the Tony I knew, understanding and kind.

"Good point." Had I overreacted?

He squeezed my hand and trailed kisses along my neck, stopped right below my ear to wrench a soft moan from my throat. He leaned his forehead against mine, his eyes capturing mine. "If I came on too strong about your niece, I apologize. Am I forgiven?"

"Yes."

He kissed the tip of my nose and winked. In that instant the remaining tension between us slipped away.

Once he released his hold, I twisted spaghetti onto my fork and took a bite. "Hmmm-mmmm, you've outdone yourself."

"You haven't seen anything yet. Just wait until you get me into bed," he said, winking and raising my temperature several degrees.

I touched his hand, ran a finger along his wrist. "Spend tonight with me. Summer doesn't need to know, and even if she finds out, we're adults."

"I'd like to…what the hell. I'm all yours."

I wondered why he'd hesitated, but since he chose that moment to kiss me, the question slipped my mind.

Just for tonight I'd forget about Summer and her troubles. Just for tonight, I'd concentrate on Tony. On us.

Some time later while Tony loaded the dishwasher,

I filled a plate for Summer and took it upstairs but was surprised to find her room empty.

She wasn't in the bathroom, and her window was locked from inside so I knew she hadn't climbed out.

Had she run away?

I spotted the plastic bag bulging with her possessions so I knew she'd return because I couldn't imagine she'd leave her clothing behind.

Where was she? And why hadn't she told me she was going out for a while?

I left the plate of spaghetti on the nightstand and rushed downstairs. I looked all over the house, checked out back and stuck my head out the front door but didn't see Summer. I called her name, but she didn't reply.

Please let her be all right.

Dread thickened a lump in my throat.

I dashed into the kitchen where Tony was washing a pan. He turned and dropped the dishcloth into the sink. "Babe, what's wrong?"

"Summer's gone. I searched every room, and she's not in the house."

He wiped his hands on a towel. "Take it easy. She can't have gone far."

"She was depressed. What if something's happened to her?"

Terrible scenarios flashed through my mind. My pulse quickened.

Tony squeezed my hand. "I'll grab my coat and go look for her."

"Should I call the police?

"First, let me check out the neighborhood."

An explosion shook the house. The sound of splintering wood and twisting metal rent the air.

Both of us ran into the garage. I flipped on the overhead lights.

As if in slow motion I took in the destruction. The busted garage door, Tony's Porsche, its fenders dented and warped, the mangled front bumper rammed into my Volvo. I heard Tony's curses, saw the startled look on Summer's face behind the deflated air bag.

I hurried to the driver's door. "Are you hurt?"

"I don't think so."

"Is anything broken? Did you bang your head? Make sure you can move your arms and legs. Maybe I should call 911."

"Calm down, Annie," Tony said, his jaw stiff and unyielding. "I'm sure she'll live to destroy someone else's car."

"I don't appreciate your sarcasm."

"Can you blame me?"

Yes.

No.

I no longer knew what I thought.

It took Tony and me several minutes before we could free my niece. When she finally stepped out of the car, looking upset but fine, I was both relieved and furious.

"Are you sure you're all right?" I asked.

"I'll live."

I wanted to shake her. "What were you thinking?"

"She wasn't thinking," Tony shouted.

She shook her head and sent him a frightened glance. "I didn't mean to do it."

"Stay away from me," he said. "Don't even talk to me right now."

"I'm sorry. It was an accident," Summer said, her voice breaking.

Tony's face twisted with rage. "This…is no accident. You deliberately stole my keys and started my car."

She dashed a trembling hand across her eyes. "I already said I was sorry."

Ignoring her, he surveyed the damage from all angles. "How in the hell did you manage to dent the back bumper, too?"

Tears ran down her face. "I just wanted to back it up a few feet, but it stalled."

I rested my hand on Summer's arm. At least she was taking responsibility for her actions.

"So how in the hell did my Porsche end up crashing into the garage?"

"I figured you might not notice the tiny dent on the back bumper if I put it back the exact place where you'd parked it. But I had trouble using the clutch and the brake. The stupid car jerked forward and slammed into the garage door."

Tony shot her a lethal look.

"Don't make a federal case. I said I'd pay you back so what's the big deal?"

A humorless laugh tore from his throat. "You can't afford the repairs. You stole my car, that's what the big deal is."

"Tony, you don't have to yell. She didn't mean it," I said.

"Like hell she didn't. The little bitch did this on purpose."

Little bitch.

That word again.

Summer was bawling so hard she could barely catch her breath.

I understood why Tony was upset, but he was the adult. It was only a car, granted an expensive car, but cars could be repaired or replaced. Summer could not deal with more verbal abuse.

A hollow ache settled in my gut. "Tony, please tell Summer you didn't mean that."

"Are you nuts? I meant every word."

My insides went numb. "I'd like you to leave."

Without a word, he slammed back into my house and called a cab.

On his way out, he brushed past me; we exchanged cold looks before he jumped into the cab.

* * *

Some time later a wrecker arrived and put Tony's car on a flatbed. The mechanic helped me pry open the garage door so I could get my vehicle out.

Afterward I went up to Summer's room. The door was opened so I slipped inside and saw her sitting on the bed, crying, her arms hanging down between her legs.

"I really blew it this time," she said, as I neared.

"You sure did."

"What are you gonna do to me?"

I'd asked myself the same question. I couldn't allow Summer to go unpunished, but hadn't she been punished enough in her young life? "You need to learn to respect other people's property. You had no business taking Tony's keys."

She sniffed and wiped her eyes with a tissue she'd pulled from her pocket. "Are you gonna lecture me?"

"You have it coming to you, but no, I have no intention of ranting so you can tune me out. I will say this, however, if you were my daughter I'd ground you for a gazillion years."

"So, do it," she said, her cold gaze daring me.

"But since you won't be staying here long enough, I've decided to ground you for five days. Which means you won't be allowed to visit Carrie or her boys."

"But we had plans."

"You'll have to cancel them."

"That's not fair."

"That's unfortunate."

"You pretend to care about me, but you don't."

"You know that's not true. If I didn't love you, you wouldn't be living with me right now. The sooner you learn there are repercussions to your actions, the better your life will be."

"That's a bunch of crap."

"What you did tonight wasn't fair to Tony."

"You're just like everybody else. You are *so* unfair."

I tried not to flinch. "I can't help the way you feel. And while we're discussing what's fair and what isn't, I want you to know that Tony was wrong to call you the *B* word."

"That's no big deal. My mom's called me lots worse."

This time, I did flinch. "Anyway, it wasn't right for him to call you that."

"I can't believe you're sticking up for me after what I've done."

"I don't condone what you did, but neither do I condone Tony calling you names."

Summer leaned back against the bed. "If I can't go to Carrie's house then I won't get paid any babysitting money. How do you expect me to make it up to Tony?"

"All I want is for you to give him a sincere apology."

"I already said I was sorry."

"Well, you're going to say it again and this time, sound like you mean it."

"That is *so* unfair."

"Your callous actions caused a lot of anger and hurt tonight. Instead of you thinking about yourself, I want you to focus on that."

Summer was still muttering about how her life sucked when I left her room and called Vi to ask if she could stay with Summer while I went out. When she showed up a few minutes later, I explained what had happened to the garage door. I was relieved that she didn't ask questions about where I was going at this time of night.

A few minutes later I turned onto the Gray, New Gloucester exit and took the Maine Turnpike toward Saco. I'd get no sleep tonight if I didn't speak to Tony. The rift between us had widened.

Once he stormed out my door, I wondered if the accident had done irreparable harm to our relationship.

As I ran the evening's events through my mind, I realized I'd sided with Summer. From Tony's perspective it might appear as though I'd chosen my niece over him. She'd been wrong to take his keys without permission. She'd been wrong about calling him names and being rude to him. She'd been wrong a lot lately, but calling her a bitch was wrong, too. She needed to know I was there for her no matter what.

Standing by Tony and berating Summer would have proven that I loved her only when she behaved. Love should be unconditional. Plus no amount of shouting, name calling and belittling would undo the damage to his car. Once I talked to Tony, I hoped he'd understand my side. In the grand scheme of things, the accident could have been a lot worse. No one was hurt. Once Tony had had a chance to calm down, I was sure he'd agree.

Plus, he had good insurance coverage, and I'd pay his deductible. The accident was more of an inconvenience, a small ding on the road of life.

I was certain Summer had learned a valuable lesson. I was also certain that once I'd had a chance to talk to Tony, he'd see it my way. Accidents happen all the time. Granted, Summer had deliberately driven the Porsche, but she hadn't intentionally crashed it into the garage.

It had been an accident.

So why was I so nervous about confronting Tony?

Because he'd waited a long time to buy that Porsche—his pride and joy. Because I remembered the nasty, obstinate look on his face when he'd left my house....

CHAPTER 13

As I drove on the highway, I began to calm down and think of all the good times I'd had with Tony. I still saw hope in our relationship, not while Summer lived with me, but after she went back home.

He hadn't wanted children. Neither had I. In truth, I'd gone along with him because at the time, I'd realized I loved Tony too much to say goodbye, and my window of opportunity for bearing children was now open only a crack.

But the way he'd interacted with Summer had shown me flaws I hadn't known existed. Tony, the generous, caring man I'd fallen in love with could also be an insensitive bastard. Though it would take a while for me to deal with this revelation, I was willing to work on our relationship, in hopes of finding what we'd lost.

About a mile from Tony's house, I phoned Vi. "Hi, did I get any calls?" Translated, had Tony called. He should have cooled down by now, and I assumed he felt as bad as I did about the way we'd parted.

"No."

"Is everything okay there?" I asked, trying not to sound disappointed.

"Everything's fine, dear. I checked up on Summer a few minutes ago and offered her some hot chocolate. She'd stopped crying. Were you expecting a call?"

"Not really, I just thought I'd check." Maybe Tony and I had crossed paths. Maybe he'd gone back to my place. Maybe he wouldn't be home, and we'd laugh about it later when we finally connected.

Or maybe he didn't love me as much as I'd thought he did.

"Good night dear, don't worry about a thing."

"Thanks again, Vi."

Shortly after eleven, I pulled into Tony's driveway. A dim light flickered inside the living room. I shut the door to my Volvo, walked up the front steps and rang the doorbell. Then I remembered his doorbell hadn't worked the last time I visited so I knocked. I had my own key but didn't want to surprise anyone, especially a roommate with a possible date.

I knocked louder and peeked in through the small slit in the drapes, saw several candles on the coffee table along with a bottle of wine and two glasses. I waited a moment, took another look in the window and spotted Tony wearing only his silk pajama bottoms, the ones I'd bought him for his birthday, the ones we often shared after we'd made love. The only explanation that came to mind was that he'd anticipated my visit. He'd called

Vi, and though I hadn't told her where I was going, she'd guessed. Though she hadn't asked, I was certain she suspected. I gave her credit for being so diplomatic.

I tapped on the window. Tony turned and focused in my direction. He looked upset, nervous. Thinking he hadn't seen me, I rapped my knuckles against the glass.

"Tony, it's Annie."

"Annie," I heard him say, his muffled voice sounding strange. I thought I heard him curse.

Why would he curse?

I watched him hurry toward the door. The deadbolt clicked, and the door opened. "Annie, why are you here?"

Because I'm confused, and we need to talk.

"Because I'm so sorry about what happened to your car. And Summer is, too."

His frown deepened.

Since I was here to mend our relationship, I decided to postpone the rest of what I'd wanted to say to him, and instead, try to recapture the magic we'd felt not so long ago.

"I love you, that's why." I circled his naked chest with eager arms and drew him against me. Never mind that it was almost forty degrees outside, I wasn't cold. But Tony should be.

Instead of pulling me inside as I'd expected, he moved onto the step, and held me tight, pushing the door behind him almost closed. "You're really something. Driving the entire way out here just to tell me you love me."

I ran my thumbnail over his nipple and felt it pebble under my touch. "I came here to talk and make sure everything is all right between us."

"Of course it is."

A slight breeze peppered his flesh with goose bumps.

"We should go inside before you catch cold," I said, nudging him toward the door.

"I'm fine, really."

"You aren't even dressed. You must be freezing."

"It's not that cold."

Warning bells went off. "Is something wrong?"

"Of course not," he replied, looking guilty as hell.

"What's going on?"

"Nothing."

"Then why are we standing on your doorstep when we could be in each others' arms in your warm, comfortable bed?"

I'd expected him to agree, rush inside and make fast work of shedding his pajama bottoms along with my clothes. Instead, Tony turned around, peered into the living room a moment, then clicked the door shut.

Looking down at me, he exhaled a long breath; a cloud of frosty air puffed from between his lips. "Babe, I'm still too angry to discuss your niece. If I let you in, we'll get into a fight, and I'm not up to that."

"For tonight that subject will be off-limits. I promise."

Tension creased his forehead and the tiny lines around his mouth and eyes. He shook his head, and putting his hands on my arms, backed me down the stairs.

"What are you doing?"

"Escorting you to your car.

"Tomorrow when you've had a chance to think, you'll realize I'm doing this for us," he said, his lips brushing the side of my face as I glared at him.

"Don't you dare tell me how I'm going to feel in the morning."

"I'm not changing my mind," he said, his voice soft but firm, as he rushed me toward the driver's door.

He stopped for a moment to eye the broken taillight on my Volvo.

I didn't want to leave, but for fear of sounding pathetic, I said nothing and walked alongside him.

"It's for the best," he said, as though he were speaking to a small child. "I'll call you later, and we can talk. But I want some distance between us when we discuss the accident. You know how important that car was to me." He opened the driver's door and rested a hand on top of my head as though concerned I might bump it while getting in.

Exasperated, I sat down and swung my legs under the dashboard.

He leaned in and gave me a hurried kiss. "Be careful driving, and—

The outside light came on.

"Sweetie, what are you doing out there?"

I turned the same instant he did, heard him gasp.

As if in slow motion, my mind processed the details. The woman clothed in Tony's silk pajama top, the top three buttons undone, the swell of her breast, the shapely legs beneath the smooth fabric, tangled hair ruffled by a lover.

Realization struck. Hard.

I swallowed back a cry, turned disbelieving eyes toward Tony.

His lips were parted as though he were ready to defend himself, yet unsure what to say. Guilt marred his otherwise handsome face. I shuddered in disbelief, my heart thudding like a lead weight against my ribs.

"Let's talk about this," he said.

I slammed the door shut, shoved the key in the ignition and backed out of the driveway, tires screeching.

I'd driven about five miles when I spotted a pickup truck behind me, flashing its high beams. When the vehicle passed, the driver tooted the horn, and I caught a glimpse of Tony behind the wheel. He motioned for me to pull over.

I steered my car along the shoulder of the road and watched him pull behind me. As he strode to the passenger side, I opened the window.

"We need to talk," he said, urgency in his tone.

"There's nothing to talk about."

"Dammit, there's everything to talk about. I want a chance to explain. You owe me that much."

"I owe you nothing."

I noticed he'd thrown on jeans and a wrinkled short sleeve shirt. He looked haggard.

And desperate.

He ran his hand through his hair. "I don't blame you for being angry. Let me follow you to your house and we can talk there?"

"No way."

"Then meet me at the Burger King a mile down the road and give me a chance to try to make things right between us."

"There's no point…."

"We love each other. Please, don't let it end this way."

"All right, I'll meet you, but I won't listen to any more lies."

"No lies, I promise."

So I followed him into the parking lot of the fast-food restaurant situated along the Maine Turnpike. I parked my car several spaces away from his. As I watched him walk toward me, I tried to imagine a plausible excuse for what I'd seen.

Only one explanation rang true.

For a moment I sat behind the wheel, chilled, a familiar hollow ache festering inside.

Tony opened my door. Startled me. Where had he come from? Then I remembered.

"Annie, let's go inside. It's too cold to talk out here."

"It wasn't so cold a few minutes ago." I wouldn't allow him to touch me. Instead I marched on stiff legs, keeping a safe distance. He led me to a corner booth, away from the man mopping the floor. While he went to the counter to order cups of coffee, I escaped to the bathroom. As I leaned against the counter and looked at myself in the mirror, I recognized the pathetic fool looking back at me.

Paul had made a fool of me. Tony had, too. What did that say about me? Was I so desperate to find someone to love that I'd chosen another cheating son of a bitch?

I inhaled a shuddering breath and kept my tears at bay. There'd be plenty of time to cry later, but right now, I needed to be strong, to look him in the eye and hide my emotions.

I splashed water on my face and patted it dry with a paper towel. How would I get through the next few minutes? On legs ready to give way, I managed to walk to the booth where Tony waited, his face grave.

Was that love I saw in his eyes?

How could that be?

If love hurt this much, I'd live without it.

As I neared, he jumped to his feet. He went to take my arm, but I jerked away, sent him a guarded look.

He lowered his hand. "You had me worried. If you hadn't come out soon, I was going to ask someone to go in and check on you."

I sat down, watched a drop of water slide down the foam cup. I wrapped my fingers around the cup, trying to draw from its warmth. Cold gripped me, turned my insides to ice.

"Annie, look at me."

I cast a quick glance at Tony.

"I didn't mean to hurt you," he said, for a moment his eyes tearing. "If you called me a bastard and told me to go to hell, you'd have every right. But please don't do that. Please don't let this ruin what we've got. I want another chance."

"I thought you loved me."

"I never stopped loving you." He reached for my hand.

I pulled away and grabbed a sugar packet, tore off the top and poured it into my cup. I dumped in two creamers and watched the white swirl blend with the brown liquid. When I could no longer put off looking at Tony again, I forced myself to meet his gaze, held it as though I were strong.

I'd loved those eyes, his mouth, his hands, his knuckles sprinkled with brown hair. For a moment, I remembered how intimately those fingers knew every inch of me.

My insides crumbled, but I held fast.

"You slept with her."

A subtle nod.

I didn't even blink.

The muscles in his jaw flexed. "But she doesn't mean a thing to me."

I cringed. "Give me some credit."

"I mean it."

"Who is she?"

"She rents my house."

"How convenient. You never even bothered to tell me your tenant was a woman."

"It didn't seem important. I don't blame you for being upset."

"Upset doesn't even begin to describe how I feel."

"Try to understand."

Fighting back tears, I stared at him. "What's to understand? You screwed her."

"Don't, babe…"

"Do you call her 'babe,' too?"

"I was upset, arrived at my house in a rage. She tried to comfort me, and one thing led to another."

"Don't make this sound spur-of-the-moment. You lit candles and drank wine." Another thought repulsed me. "It's not the first time, is it?"

He had the decency to glance away. "I was weak, and…she was there."

I was weak, and she was there.

Had that been Paul's reasoning, too?

"I'm leaving," I said, my voice steady and calm.

"I'm coming with you. I don't want you driving while you're upset."

"You're worried about me now? It's a bit late for that. And just for the record Summer isn't a bitch."

"I'm sorry about that. I was upset. I didn't know what I was saying. I'll call you tomorrow."

"Don't call. Don't bother to show up at my door. I never want to see you again." My insides trembled so much I was shocked I could even speak.

Pain flooded his face.

And my heart.

I pushed myself up. My legs held. I wanted to scream, scrape my fingernails down his face.

Instead, I walked away.

CHAPTER 14

The following Saturday Vi arrived early, ready to tutor my niece.

I poured coffee into two cups. "I sure hope you can get through to her. I tried helping her with her homework this week, but she just doesn't seem to care. She sits with her arms folded, looking confused, and at times, even refuses to look at the book. She says she's tired, or she just doesn't get it. She keeps repeating she's stupid, and that nothing sinks into her thick skull. Her teachers say she's becoming more withdrawn and doesn't take part in class discussions."

"I'll do my best to figure out a plan of attack. But much of this will depend on Summer."

"I'm not giving up."

"Neither will I. How are things going with the school psychologist?"

"She's not cooperating with her either."

I lifted my cup and paused. "If we can prove to Summer that she's smart, then maybe she'll leave here with a better attitude and be willing to continue being tutored after she returns home."

"If there's a way to teach that child, I'll find it," Vi said with confidence, giving me hope. "Since we have so little time left, how do you feel about pulling her out of the school system and letting me work with her full-time."

"Can we do that?"

"Sure, lots of people with no qualifications homeschool their children. I have a master's in education for goodness' sake, that should count for something. If it's all right with you, I'll check on it first thing Monday."

"Let's ask Summer what she thinks."

"It's not up to her to decide. We're the adults."

"I want to give her a choice. I get the feeling no one has ever asked for her opinion before."

I could tell Vi wasn't convinced. "In my day, kids did what they were told."

"But orders don't work with Summer. And homeschooling will work better if she feels she has a say in it."

Looking doubtful, Vi said, "Personally, I think she needs firm guidance and to be made to realize she has no choice. But we'll agree to disagree on this. Does she know I'm coming?"

"Yes, I'll tell her you're here." I hurried up the stairs and knocked on the bedroom door.

"What?"

I slid the door open. "Vi's here to help you with your schoolwork."

Summer rolled her eyes. "Tell that old bitch who thinks she knows everything to leave me the hell alone."

"You of all people should realize how hurtful that word can be."

Guilt flashed across her face.

"Vi wants what's best for you."

"Yeah, well, I don't need her help."

I stood there. "I've been very patient with you. I know you're disappointed that you're stuck here in Maine, but while you're living with me, I expect you to treat everyone with respect. So get downstairs and listen to whatever Vi tells you. She's an excellent teacher. If you work with her, your grades will shoot up."

Disbelief clouded her eyes. "Yeah, like that's ever gonna happen."

"It won't happen if you stay up here, so go. Now."

She pushed herself off the bed and with a long moan, left the bedroom and stomped down the stairs.

Wanting to give Vi and Summer some privacy, I stayed away from the kitchen. But my curiosity piqued after an hour. All I could hear were soft murmurs. Much better than the hysterics I'd expected from Summer. To amuse myself I flicked on the television. Except for an infomercial about exercise equipment guaranteed to firm every inch of me, there was little on but cartoons. So I shut off the set and dusted and vacuumed the living room, all the while trying to imagine what was being said in the other room.

Thirty minutes later Summer opened the kitchen door and continued across the room.

I couldn't read her expression. "How did it go?"

"I'm dumber than dirt."

Her attitude rankled.

Stay calm.

She's only a child.

I dropped my dust cloth. "Stop right there." I walked over to her and put my hands on her arms. "When you talk like that, you sure do sound dumb."

Shock widened her eyes. Anger raised her voice. "I wondered how long it would take you to figure that out."

"You don't even try. You talk like you were raised in the gutter. Well, I've had it. As long as you live under my roof, you're going to clean up your act. I love you, Summer, but I won't listen to you degrade yourself this way. I believe in you, but unless you believe in yourself, you don't stand a chance. So I need your help here. And you can start by speaking like a civilized human being. Do I make myself clear?"

She shrugged.

"I'd like an answer."

A wry smile curled her mouth. "You sure are bitchy since you and Tony broke up."

"Would you care to rephrase that?" I asked.

"You sure are mean since…"

"That's better. For a dumb kid, you catch on fast."

She was mumbling under her breath as she tore up the stairs. Had I handled that the right way? Once more, I realized I knew nothing about raising a teenager. Yet what I'd said felt right. And right or wrong, Summer was done putting herself down.

And yes, she was right. I'd been a royal bitch since the night I'd discovered Tony with his *roommate*. He'd dared to show his face the following morning, but I'd sent him away.

I wasn't sure about much, but this I knew without a doubt: I'd done the right thing the night I'd walked away from him.

With a heavy heart I went into the kitchen, upset with myself for allowing his memory to get me down. I planted a smile on my face when I saw Vi. "So how did it go?"

"I asked Summer how she felt about my home-schooling her. She seemed relieved she wouldn't have to return to school so that's settled. I'll spend the weekdays tutoring her, and if need be, I'll work with her on Saturday mornings, too."

"Do you think she'll cooperate with you?" I asked, doubting she would.

"She'll have to if she doesn't want to find herself back in the classroom. I think she's embarrassed to be among children her age, because they laugh at her."

"Did she say that?"

"No, I read between the lines. And kids can be so cruel." Vi glanced down at the notepad in front of her. "I know why Summer is flunking her classes."

How could she know already? Could it really be something simple?

"Summer can't read."

A wave of shock rippled through me. "How is that possible? She's in junior high."

"Lots of students slip through the cracks. If we work on her reading skills, her other grades will also improve." Vi turned a page in her tablet and looked at her notes. "I showed Summer some flash cards I'd brought along, with very basic words, and she recognized very few. But she's bright and catches on really fast. Within an hour she knew most of the words on my cards. The challenge will be to keep her interested. A child her age doesn't want to read kindergarten books. When I asked her what interested her, she said basketball. So this afternoon, I'm off to the library to check out some books about the sport."

"I called the YMCA about their basketball program, but the person in charge was on vacation this week. I'm hoping they have a team for teenagers," I said.

Vi's eyes brightened. "If so, that might give us the leverage we need. If Summer wants to play, she needs to work on her reading."

"I'd hate to do that to her. She's had so little in her life."

"You need to be firm about this. There's a lot more than a basketball game at stake here. Summer's future depends on whether she can learn to read."

"I'll let you know what I decide after I've spoken to the woman at the Y. How much do you hope to accomplish with her in the four weeks she has left here?"

"If I can keep her motivated, and if she works hard, she could be reading first or second grade level by then."

The disappointment must have shown on my face because Vi continued, "That's a major step. Once she learns the basics, there's no telling what she'll be able to accomplish. The main thing is the problem has been identified. When she returns home, I'll speak with her tutor and explain the program I'm using. With the help of a dedicated teacher, I'm convinced Summer can bring her reading skills up to her grade level within a year, possibly six months. That's if she sticks to it and doesn't give up."

That Friday afternoon, I'd decided to skip meeting my friends at DiMillo's because I didn't want Vi to think I was taking advantage of her generosity. When Vi found out, she insisted that I go. According to her, Summer would benefit from their extra hour together. More important, she hoped the time with friends would help chase away my gloomy disposition.

I arrived a little late. Mallory had already ordered dessert and drinks.

I sat down and slid my purse under the table. "How's it going?"

Carrie replied, "Great, except my boys want to know when Summer can come play with them again."

"She's been pretty busy with Vi, but I'd hoped to drop over this weekend, that's if you aren't too busy."

"Sure, plan on having breakfast at my house."

"That'll be fun. I'll stop at the bakery."

Carrie lifted a hand in protest. "Don't do that. I'm on a diet again."

Mallory laughed. "What else is new?"

Carrie took a sip of water. "Easy for you to laugh. You're tall and were born with skinny genes. Both my parents are short, and my mother gets wider each year. It's a battle, but this time I'm sticking to it."

Carrie wasn't heavy by any means, but she did carry an extra stubborn fifteen pounds on her hips. "Then I'll bring along doughnuts for the kids, and some fruit, cottage cheese and bagels for us," I said.

"Deal," Carrie replied with a smile. "You don't look so good."

"You look like hell. Have you heard from Tony?" Mallory asked.

"He's called several times, but I've hung up on him."

Carrie shook her head. "Have you thought of giving him another chance?"

Carrie's suggestion didn't surprise me. In the past, she'd given the men she'd dated too many chances. But the thought of Tony's betrayal knotted my insides. "A chance for what? To cheat on me again?"

"He said he was sorry," Carrie said.

"Not as sorry as I was to find him playing house with his roommate."

Mallory tapped my arm. "I say good riddance. Don't give that bastard the opportunity to knife you in the back again."

Nicely phrased. The pain of his betrayal had cut deeply.

Bitterness clogged the back of my throat. "Anyway, according to Vi, I need my spirits lifted."

"You've come to the right place," Mallory said, tapping a manicured fingernail against the linen tablecloth. "Maybe I can ask John if he has a friend you can borrow for a night or two." Mallory wiggled her eyebrows. "I'm told there's nothing like a night of hot sex to erase old memories."

My lips curved into an easy smile. "Yeah, great idea."

"Better still, how about two guys. At once," she continued her eyes wide and animated.

Carrie giggled. "I can barely handle one man. What would I do with two?"

"No, no, it's not what you'd do, but what they could do for you," Mallory said, laughing and trying, I suspected, to shock Carrie, which wasn't difficult.

"In that case, tell John to line up three of his friends. I have some serious memories to erase," I said, and then assured Carrie I was only joking.

The three of us laughed like schoolgirls, and when I dug into my chocolate cake, I really did feel better. "How's it going with John?"

Mallory's pensive expression said it all.

"Uh-oh," Carrie said. "Another one…on his way out the door."

"What's that no-good jerk done to you?" I asked, expecting to hear something terrible.

For a moment, Mallory seemed at a loss for words. "He knows how strongly I feel, yet he broke my first commandment of dating."

"There are dating commandments?" Carrie said. "No wonder I'm not getting anywhere. What are they?"

"I wouldn't even dare venture a guess," I said.

Mallory ran her tongue over her lower lip. "He's ruined what we had. Anyway, I don't want to talk about it. We're here to cheer up Annie."

"Maybe we should be cheering you up," I said, wondering how Mallory could look so carefree. I wished I could be more like her.

"Doesn't it make you sad to know it's over?" Carrie asked.

Mallory ran her fingernail over the condensation of her water glass. "That's why I keep my relationships simple. Nothing to weigh me down. I told John when we first started going out that it was a temporary arrangement, a fling, no strings attached. And he'd said he had to be the luckiest man in the world. So I'm moving on. I'll look back fondly on the times we've shared together."

"How does John feel about it?" Carrie asked.

"He doesn't know yet."

"Shouldn't you be talking to him instead of us?" I asked.

"I plan to tell him this evening," Mallory replied with a hollow ring to her voice. "He's a good-looking guy. He won't have any trouble finding another woman, someone willing to settle down and have his babies."

From that comment, I assumed John had wanted a committed relationship. It was ironic. Mallory would send John away because he cared too much.

I'd broken up with Tony because he didn't care enough.

I arrived home and thanked Vi for staying late.

"The time with your friends did you some good," Vi said. "It's nice to see a smile on your face. I left Summer's papers on the table for you to see. She's starting to take a little pride in her accomplishments. However, she's fighting me every step of the way."

"I hope she isn't being rude."

"She's doing somewhat better with that, dear. And she's allowing me to teach her the material, but she's not working hard. As a matter of fact, she's barely working at all. Yet even with her halfhearted effort,

I'm amazed at how much she's learned in a short while."

"That's encouraging, right?"

"Somewhat, but she's not doing the assignments I give her. I need to find some incentive to motivate her."

"I'll talk to her. The YMCA coach called today to say the basketball team starts practicing next Monday. I've decided to go along with your suggestion. I'm going to tell Summer that if she wants to play basketball, she'll have to do her homework."

"That may be all the push she needs."

I bit down on my lower lip. "We'll know soon enough."

Some time later, I went upstairs to speak to Summer. She was on the bed watching MTV. I considered discussing trivial issues before tackling what I had in mind. But I decided to jump right in.

"Vi says you're making progress with your schoolwork."

She stared at the screen. I may have detected an almost unperceivable nod, but I wasn't sure.

"She says you aren't doing your assignments."

She rolled her eyes. "You just don't get it. I told you I'm too dumb."

"Vi thinks you aren't trying hard enough. She thinks you're very smart, but not willing to work."

Another roll of her eyes. "I get sick of writing down

the same words over and over and over again. Borrr-rrring."

"Since you're tired of boring, I have some exciting news for you."

"Yeah, what?"

"The Y has a basketball team looking for a few good players."

She swung her feet over the edge of the bed. "Really?"

"Yes. They start practice on Monday."

"Can I go?"

"Only if you do the assignments Vi gives you."

"I can't. The letters get all jumbled up, and nothing makes sense."

"You aren't being fair to Vi or to yourself when you do a shoddy job of your schoolwork. You have a choice. If you want to play basketball, you do your homework."

"You are *so* unfair."

Later that night, I heard a knock on the door. I peeked outside and saw Tony's truck parked in the driveway. My heart thudded wildly.

Raw pain sliced through me. I considered not opening the door, but before I could decide, I heard a key in the lock.

"Annie." Tony walked inside, shut the door and started toward me.

Every muscle in my body tensed. "That's close enough."

Pain clouded his eyes. "We were so good together."

"We aren't anymore."

The lines on his face were more pronounced than I'd remembered, as though he hadn't slept in days.

"I can't stop thinking about you. I want to come back."

"No."

"That's it, just no."

"We've already gone through this. Before you go, take the rest of your things that I boxed up and put in the garage. And leave your keys. You don't need them anymore."

"If it wasn't for that little bit—"

"Don't even go there."

"Well it's true. If it wasn't for that kid, none of this would have happened. She not only wrecked my Porsche, she tore us apart."

I hurried across the room and opened the door.

"Don't you dare blame Summer for what's happened to us. Now get out."

CHAPTER 15

After a sleepless night, I sat in the kitchen in my nightgown and robe, sipping a cup of cold coffee. I'd known things were over between Tony and me, but last night had once more driven the point home. What a fool I'd been.

I'd thought we'd be together forever.

I'd thought he loved me enough to be faithful.

Wrong again.

I heard the door behind me open and shut. I caught a glimpse of blond hair and a red stripe. I jerked my head around and stared in disbelief at Summer who wore no makeup. "What did you do to your hair and your face?"

"I could ask you the same thing. You look terrible."

"I had trouble sleeping last night, and I haven't been near a comb. Now you?"

She shrugged. "I ran out of black hair spray."

"You mean that wasn't permanent color?"

"You think I'm a moron or something? No way I'd dye my hair black for good. Anyway, the color didn't work the way I'd intended. Nothing did."

"What's that mean?"

"You were supposed to take one look at me at the airport in my Goth getup and put me on the next plane heading to L.A. I'd planned to go back and hang out with my friends. But it was a waste of time. So there's no point in me continuing this charade."

She sure sounded like a smart kid.

"You aren't Goth?"

"Of course not. My mom's friend, Gwen, is. People freak out when they see her. And that's before she opens her mouth and starts with all the morbid stuff. I figured that gloomy look would work for me, but I'm still here...."

"Is the red stripe more hair spray?"

"Nope, the red is cool. So now that you know, can I stop seeing that shithead at the school?"

I didn't have the energy to criticize her speech.

Plus, it took a moment for me to realize she meant the therapist. "You aren't seeing the therapist because I thought you were Goth. You're seeing her because I thought it would be good for you to have someone to talk to."

"We don't talk, she does. I mostly tune her out."

"Let me think about it."

"Please don't take too long, because I can't take much more of her."

"I'll give you an answer tomorrow."

She glanced down at her black boots and shuffled

her foot back and forth. "Next time you see Tony, tell him I'm really sorry, and I'm gonna pay to fix his car."

"I've already mailed him a check to cover his deductible."

"I wrecked everything."

"You damaged his car, big deal." When I realized what I'd said, I added, "Well, it is a big deal, I don't want you to think you can take other people's property without asking. Tony should eventually get over it. And if not, then that's his problem."

"He sure freaked out when he saw what I'd done."

"Don't you think he had good reason?"

She nodded, pulled a chair close to me and sat down. "Once he gets his car back, I bet he'll be in a good mood again, just like before."

"I don't know."

And I don't care to know.

Tony was out of my life for good. I might still feel the raw ache inside at the mention of his name, but there was no turning back.

Summer touched my shoulder. "I wish you didn't look so sad."

The gesture was so sweet.

So sincere.

So loving.

I started to cry.

That Friday Vi arrived early so I could leave for work.

I knew instantly something was wrong. "Are you feeling sick?"

"I have one of my migraines starting, but I should be fine in a little while."

"Do you want me to stay home?"

"That's not necessary. I'll give Summer an assignment and lie down for a while. I've already taken my medication. Give me a couple hours rest, and I'll be good as new."

"Are you sure?" I hated to leave with her feeling like this.

"Summer can take care of herself, and she has plenty to keep her occupied. She has some worksheets she can do while I recuperate. I might even ask her to brew me a cup of tea."

I worked until noon. I didn't dare call for fear of waking Vi. Besides, if she needed my help, she'd call.

But I could wait no longer. So I dialed my number. It rang six times before Vi answered, sounding groggy. "Mrs. Annie Jacobs' residence, Violet Jacobs speaking."

"Vi, how are you feeling?"

"I dozed off. But I think my headache's gone." She paused a moment. "Yes, it's gone. I can't believe I slept this long. I hear the television in the next room so Summer must be done with the assignments I gave her."

"I won't keep you. I'm glad you're feeling better."

"Thank the good Lord for that."

* * *

Twenty minutes later, intending to go out for lunch with my coworkers, I took my purse, put on my coat and was ready to leave when the phone rang.

Roberta ran into the office. "Your mother-in-law's on line one. She sounds as though she's crying."

I hurried across the room and picked up the receiver. "What's wrong?"

"Summer's gone," Vi said.

"Gone where?"

"I don't know, but she isn't here. I've checked every room in the house. I even looked around outside."

"I'll be right there," I said. "Call my cell if you hear from her."

I took the elevator down to the lobby, ran through the parking garage and jumped into the car. I didn't remember the ride home or paying for the tolls, but I somehow managed to arrive safely.

Vi met me at the door. "Thank the Lord you're here."

"Have you heard from her?"

"No. I could never live with myself if anything happened to that child while she was under my watch."

"It's not your fault," I said, walking past Vi into the house.

She shut the door, took a lace hankie from her pocket and dashed away tears. "After you left this morning, my head felt like it was ready to split open. Of course that's no excuse, but when I discovered that

Summer hadn't done the homework assignment I'd given her, I blew up. I called her lazy. I told her she could forget about basketball because she didn't deserve to play."

"What did she say to that?"

"She told me to go screw myself."

"Damn, I thought we were making progress."

"Oh, but let me finish. A few minutes later, she came to me and said she was sorry. She pleaded with me to give her another chance. She swore she'd complete all her assignments while I rested if she'd be allowed to try out for the team. I apologized for shouting at her. I told Summer I'd be in the stands cheering for her at the first basketball game. I made it clear how proud I was of her progress with her reading. She looked pleased as punch. Thinking we'd smoothed everything out, I went to bed. Summer even came in a short while later to ask whether I'd like something to drink. She sounded so sincere and polite. I'd thought she was concerned for my well-being, but now I realize she was checking up on me to make sure I was staying put so she could run off."

I tried to console Vi and reassure her that she wasn't at fault for Summer's disappearance, that Summer would arrive any minute and all would be back to normal. Or as normal as life could be while Summer lived under my roof.

I checked the house again and even called the school though I doubted she'd go there. Then I walked around the block and spoke to a few of my neighbors, but no one had seen her. I phoned Carrie and Mallory, but they had no idea where Summer might be.

At 1:00, Vi asked, "Shouldn't we call the police, dear?"

"I think we should wait. Summer wouldn't run away without taking her clothes. Everything she owns is still in her bedroom."

"It's all my fault. If only I hadn't yelled at her."

"Vi, stop blaming yourself. Summer's not a defenseless toddler. She acted without thinking of the consequences."

"Yes, but she's still a child. I should have known better than to take my eyes off her."

"How were you to know?"

"If only I hadn't gone to bed."

"You were sick. Stop beating yourself up over this. Besides, Summer will probably walk through the door any minute and give us some lame excuse."

"I sure hope so."

"Me, too." Unfortunately the possible scenarios running through my head frightened me.

At 1:30 I called the hospitals, but the emergency room nurses assured me that they'd seen no one fitting Summer's description.

At 1:35 Vi again asked, "It's been a long time. Shouldn't we call the police?"

"I hate involving the authorities. What would I tell

them? Summer's only been missing for a few hours. Her things are still here so I know she's coming back."

Was I sure of that?

I wasn't sure of anything.

I paced across the living room. Every few minutes I stopped to peer out the window, hoping to see her coming up the walk.

Staring blankly at the screen, Vi flipped through the cable channels a few times. With a frustrated sigh, she shut off the television, put down the remote and stood. "I'll boil some water for tea and get us each a little something to eat."

"I haven't even touched the last cup you brought out."

"That's cold," she said, whisking the china cup from the table and glancing wistfully at the delicate painted roses. "It's a darn shame that Paul isn't here. He'd know what to do."

I sensed she was going to talk further. Unable to deal with his memory and hoping to avoid an unpleasant discussion, I said, "While you're in the kitchen, would you mind bringing back something to eat?"

"No problem," she said, leaving the room.

She returned a moment later with two cups and thick slices of toast with raspberry jam.

"Thanks." As I picked up the bread and took one tiny bite, my stomach clenched.

I thought of the news reports I'd watched about sexual predators and drunken drivers, of people hit and left to die on the side of the road.

Had Summer taken off because she was angry as Vi suspected, or had she planned this for a while? And why would she leave her things behind?

I thought of the cases of child abduction I'd seen on the news, the tearful parents pleading for the return of their child.

"Aren't you going to eat, dear?"

"I don't think I can."

"Neither can I. At the time, a piece of toast really appealed to me." She sighed and stared out the window. "I should have never left her alone. It's because of me she's run off. I'm a teacher with years of experience. I know better than to shout at a student. I just don't know what came over me."

"Summer can stretch anyone's patience. I don't blame you. She's also thirteen and doesn't need to be watched every minute."

"In my heart, I feel responsible."

Once more I checked the clock—2:00. "I can't wait any longer. I'm calling the police."

A black-and-white cruiser pulled into my driveway. I watched a police officer step out of the car and approach my house.

I opened the door before he had a chance to knock. "I'm glad you're here."

He was over six feet tall, a commanding presence in a dark blue uniform, his shirt pulled taut over broad shoulders.

He tipped his head slightly. "Good day, ma'am, I'm Randall Myers, with the Portland PD."

I'd never cared for mustaches, but his fit his rugged features. Stepping aside, I let him pass and motioned for him to sit on a nearby chair. I sat opposite him on the couch next to Vi.

He pulled a small tablet from his pocket.

"What's the child's name, age and description?"

After I answered his questions, I realized Summer could have changed her appearance again. "Now that I think of it, she might have blond or black hair. I guess it could be any color that comes in a spray can or a bottle of dye. Oh, and her hair has a red stripe. So that should be easy to spot."

I'd expected him to react, but he didn't. Instead he continued to take notes.

"And at times, she looks Goth. Do you know what that is?" I asked, because I hadn't until Summer had arrived.

"Yes, I've had a lot of experience with Goth teens. Some of them are very troubled, but many are just typical teenagers. Over the years I've discovered really great kids beneath those garish disguises. Some people aren't willing to take the time to get to know them."

Like Tony.

I was upset with myself for conjuring his image when I should be concentrating on Summer.

"Everything she owns is still in her room. She wouldn't leave without her things. If you'd seen the way she was clutching the bag she was carrying when she first got here, you'd know she's coming back."

"Did she seem especially depressed lately?" Randall asked.

His question jolted me.

Vi had shown me articles about the high suicide rate in Goth teens.

But Summer wouldn't...

Maybe she hadn't taken her things because...she'd no longer needed them.

My insides convulsed. "What are you getting at?"

He cast a sympathetic glance toward me before turning back to his notepad. "I didn't mean to imply."

"Summer has a lot to be depressed about. Her mother overdosed on cocaine and almost died. My niece was the one who found her. She was forced to leave her home and come stay with me where she knows no one. But there's no way she'd—" My throat closed, and I couldn't continue.

Vi placed her hand over mine and faced Randall. "If I hadn't shouted at the child this morning, none of this would have happened."

"You're both being too hard on yourselves. And don't go letting your imaginations run wild," he said, in a soothing baritone, his empathetic gaze locking with mine. "If teenagers ran away every time someone raised their voice, there'd be very few of them living at home. Most kids take off and quickly realize their mistake. They return in a few hours sorry for causing their parents so much grief."

As he spoke, I noticed a small horizontal scar along his forehead, above compassionate blue eyes that put me at ease.

"Anyway, Summer isn't really a Goth," I added, feeling much better.

"Are you sure of that, dear?" Vi asked.

"Of course I'm sure. She'd have no reason to lie about that."

"I guess you're right." Vi dashed a tear away with the back of her hand.

"Do you have a recent picture of your niece?" he asked, turning to me.

"I don't," I replied, and felt like even more of a failure as an aunt. She was my only niece. I should have had lots of pictures of her, of us. But I'd been too busy with my life, with Tony, with Summer's schooling to take the time to have fun with her.

When she returned, that would change.

If she returned.

Don't even go there.

It was important to me that he understood my niece. "Since leaving L.A., everything that matters has been taken away from Summer. I'm telling you this so that when you find her, you won't judge her too harshly."

"Nothing shocks me," he said. "I've pretty much seen and heard it all."

"She'll most likely swear at you and act as though she doesn't care, but she'll be frightened."

When he smiled, his mustache swept across his lower lip. "I won't handcuff her if that's what you're worried about."

"She's really a wonderful girl," I added.

"She has good examples to emulate," he said, smiling at both of us.

"She just needs a break," I said, blinking back tears. "No one's given her a chance."

He stood, ran his fingers through thick blond hair in need of a trim. "I'll call this information into the precinct and put out an attempt to locate. The dispatchers will broadcast Summer's description to our cruisers over the radio or computer. As soon as I get the report to the dispatch center, Summer's information will be entered in the National Crime Information Center. This is a nationwide database…"

I interrupted him. "You think Summer's left the state?"

"It's just a precaution."

"But it's a possibility," I said, once more, fearing she might not be found. "And her mother, what am I supposed to tell her if she calls? That I've lost her daugh-

ter, that she shouldn't have entrusted her care to me."
I heard the desperation in my voice. "But she could
walk through that door any minute. So where is she?"

When Vi reached over and gave me a hug, I stopped
rambling.

"Chances are you're right. You know your niece better than anyone else," he said.

Did I know her at all?

He stepped toward the door. "If I hear anything, I'll
contact you immediately. I know this is rough, but
nothing will be gained by blaming yourselves. I'll do my
best to find Summer and bring her home safely."

Randall Myers exuded confidence and seemed to
genuinely care. I didn't know him, yet I trusted him.

He handed me a card with his name and the police
department's phone number. "This is in case after I
leave, you think of something else I should know."

I tucked the card in my pocket.

Vi and I watched him leave, climb into his cruiser
and drive away.

About thirty minutes later, the phone rang. I picked
up the receiver with trembling hands.

"It's Officer Randall Myers with the Portland…"

"Have you found her?"

"A teenage girl fitting Summer's description with a
red stripe in her hair is being held at Stan's Electronics at the Gray Plaza."

"Don't they know her name?"

"She won't tell them."

"Is she hurt?"

"She's fine."

The Gray Plaza, a small mall, was several miles from my house. I wondered how she'd gotten there. "Why is she being held?"

"She's been accused of shoplifting."

CHAPTER 16

When I arrived at Stan's Electronics, a woman in her late forties with black hair pulled up in tight curls ushered me inside a small office. Summer sat across the room, head down, her arms wrapped tightly around her knees drawn up on the chair.

She looked small and defenseless.

My heart gave a hollow thud.

I gripped the metal desk for support. "Summer."

She glanced up, but before she turned away and started sobbing, I saw shame on her face.

"Tell me they've made a mistake." Tell me these people are wrong, that you're not a thief. I hurried to her side and put my hand on her shoulder, which was trembling under my touch.

The scent of pine air freshener permeated the room and made my throat raw.

An overweight man with a bulbous nose and a grim-set mouth, wearing a gray suit stood up behind a desk. "I'm Stanley Bauer, owner of Stan's Electronics. There's no mistake. We caught her with the merchandise."

The woman who'd escorted me into the room nodded in agreement. "I caught her red-handed. She can't lie her way out of this."

Stanley glanced from the woman to me. "No one gets away with much on Alice's shift. She's the best we got."

"I'd better get back out there." Alice stepped toward the door and disappeared into the store.

"What happens now?" I asked, bracing for more bad news.

"The store prosecutes shoplifters. No exceptions. We've already called the police. You her mother?"

"I'm her guardian, her aunt."

"Kids like her are robbing me blind. I spend a small fortune each year on surveillance equipment and plainclothes security guards. That cost is passed on to the consumer. If I have to raise my prices much more, I'll be forced to go out of business."

"What did she take?"

"A couple of iPods. We caught her when the sensors went off as she went out the door. Once we ushered her into the office, we also found DVDs tucked in her waistband."

I noticed a *Star Wars* and a *Lord of the Rings* collector's edition on the desk and assumed those were the ones Summer had taken.

Ever so lightly, I squeezed her shoulder. "Why did you…" The word "steal" stuck in my throat. "…take these things?"

She sniffed and shook her head.

Stanley's face flushed crimson, the tiny veins on his nose more pronounced. "I'll tell you why. Either for kicks, or she probably planned to sell the loot, buy liquor and drugs and party with her friends."

"My niece doesn't do drugs." But I knew no such thing.

Summer cast a timid glance my way and gave me a wobbly smile. "I'm not stupid enough to fool around with drugs."

I believed her.

"Yet you think nothing of robbing me," Stanley said, his voice gruff.

Once more, Summer lowered her head against her knees.

I assumed Stanley would enjoy seeing Summer dragged out of his office in handcuffs. But I still had to try. "Summer will be returning to L.A. soon. Since you have your merchandise, no real harm has been done." That didn't ring true to me. I certainly didn't want my niece to get the impression that I thought stealing was all right, but I'd say whatever I had to to protect her. "I'm not trying to make light of this. Shoplifting is serious business, and I can assure you Summer will be punished. She won't cause you any more trouble. Perhaps I could pay a fine or pay for the merchandise rather than the police getting involved?"

"That would be letting her off too easily. If I did that,

pretty soon word would get out, and I'd have every crook from miles around cleaning me out."

The door to the office opened and shut. "Stanley, what have you got," came a familiar voice.

Officer Myers approached the desk. "Mind if I ask her a few questions?" His gaze focused on Summer, sitting in the fetal position, crying quietly.

"Go ahead," I replied, unsure whether he was speaking to me or Stanley.

As he knelt in front of her chair, the handcuffs on his belt clinked together. "Summer, my name's Randy Myers. I'd like to help you…if you'll let me."

Did the police handcuff children? I suspected they did when not given a choice.

Would Summer cooperate with him?

At the moment, she seemed docile, her spirit broken, but it was the other side of her that worried me— the wise-mouth kid who cursed at adults.

Stan forced a humorless laugh. "She's putting on a hell of a good act. Don't fall for all this weepy stuff. Before her aunt got here, she was telling me what I could do to myself. The kid's got a raunchy mouth, and she's not afraid to use it."

Summer's body stilled. She raised eyes filled with fury. "Beat it, cop."

My heart sank.

Randall rested his hands on the arms of the chair.

"If you refuse to cooperate, I'll have no choice but to take you in for questioning."

I wanted to fight for her, but Officer Myers already knew about her background. "Summer, he's trying to help you."

She raised piercing eyes, her face full of anger, sadness and confusion. "Yeah, right. All he wants is for me to confess so…" She sucked in a wobbly breath and aimed a despising look at Randall. "So he can finish with the case and get the hell away from me."

Randall jerked the arms of the chair and stood, his presence seeming to fill the room.

"You talk a tough game, but I don't buy it. I think you're scared. You're hiding behind a nasty attitude. As I see it, you'd better stop pretending you're something you aren't, or you'll be paying the price. If you don't work with me, you'll spend time in juvenile detention or foster care."

Blinking back tears, Summer pressed her back against the chair.

I couldn't bear the thought of my niece in foster care, or worse, juvenile detention. "Summer, talk to him. Can't you tell he's trying to help you?"

"Your aunt is worried about you, and she has good reason to be. If Stanley files those charges against you, the authorities will look up your record." Randall's voice remained calm, but filled with authority.

Stanley slammed his fist against the blotter on his desk. Paperclips flew from a small plastic disc.

Startled, I jumped.

Summer did, too.

"Damn right I'm filing charges, no ifs about it. So don't go getting it into your head that I'm letting her off."

Ignoring Stanley, Randall continued, "When they find out this isn't your first offense, you won't be going home with your aunt."

Not her first offense.

Could he be mistaken?

My doubts vanished when I saw Summer's startled expression.

A wave of disappointment rushed over me.

Did Dana know that her daughter shoplifted? Not that Dana would care or do anything about it. How could Summer become a responsible young adult if she was raised by an irresponsible mother?

"So the choice is up to you, Summer. You either talk to me right here, or I'll be forced to take you in," Randall said.

Slowly, Summer raised her chin a notch. "I did it. There, are you satisfied?"

"Tell me something I don't already know," Randall said. "Why did you steal that stuff?"

"'Cause, that's why."

"That's a cop out, and you know it."

Stanley walked around his desk and stood by Randall. "I don't care why she did it, only that she did. What difference does it make whether she's a kleptomaniac getting her jollies, or planning to exchange the loot for weed…or something stronger?"

Randall frowned at Summer. "Is that it? You do this for fun? You didn't strike me as being dumb."

"All right, I'm dumb. Now are you satisfied?"

"I want to know why you did it. Is Stan right? Were you going to buy drugs?"

Her face contorted with rage. "Never. There's no way in hell. I've seen what that shit does. I may not be very smart, but I'm not that stupid."

"Now that we've straightened that out," Randall said, "you still haven't told me what you planned to do with the stuff you stole?"

"I was going to sell it and use the money for something…important."

I squeezed her shoulder again to remind her I was still there for her. "If you needed money, you should have asked me for it."

She dashed away a stray tear. "I couldn't do that."

"Why not?"

She gulped and inhaled a ragged breath. "I wanted to pay shithead Tony for what I'd done to his car. I figured if I went to him with the money and apologized, he might come back. I wanted you to be happy again."

Guilt assailed me.

I realized I should have explained to Summer what

had happened between Tony and me so she wouldn't blame herself. As embarrassing as it was opening up in front of these two men, I needed to tell my niece how I felt.

"I don't want Tony back."

"You've been so sad lately, and I'm the one who screwed everything up."

"When you drove his Porsche into my garage, you did me a favor. Until then I'd thought Tony was perfect. The accident helped me to really see him." A *pathetic, shallow man.*

"I just wanted to make everything right again."

"Stealing is wrong," Stanley said, his tone booming.

"Where I come from, it's a necessity," Summer said, her eyes cold.

"It's not necessary while you're living with me. Tell Mr. Bauer you're sorry," I said, holding her gaze, pleading with her to apologize.

She jumped up from her chair. "You know what? You can all stop looking at me like I'm some pathetic kid. I don't give a flying crap what all of you think. It's how we do things in L.A. It's how me and my friends get some of our clothes and food. I bet none of you know what it's like to go to bed with an empty stomach."

Filled with compassion, I tried to pull her into my arms, but she pushed me away.

Stanley paced across the room. "Son of a bitch…"

Summer flattened her palms against the desk. "Anyway, my best friend, Joe, says shoplifting's not such a big deal 'cause whatever we take is covered by insurance."

Stanley jerked his head around. "And who do you think has to pay for the rise in premiums? Do I look like a wealthy man?"

I wouldn't have blamed Randall for snapping handcuffs over Summer's wrists and hauling her off. Only I hoped he didn't.

"Can't you give her a chance," I said, the words tumbling from my mouth on their own.

Meanwhile my legs were ready to collapse.

For a moment the two men focused on Summer, not blinking, not saying a word.

She stared from one to the other. Suddenly, her lower lip quivered, then she broke down and cried. "I don't know what to do anymore. Nothin' ever turns out right. I was wrong to take the stuff. I won't ever do it again. Just let me go back to Annie's house. Pleeeease."

Randall gestured for Stanley to step out of the office. After the two men left the room, I remembered the night my mother had called asking me to care for Summer. I'd never imagined being in this situation. For that matter, I'd never imagined the turmoil my life had been in the past few weeks.

Yet if I had to do it again, I'd still take her into my home. Summer had become an important part of my life. I no longer focused on the eight-year-old child I'd known, but the confused young woman she'd become.

And I loved her despite her faults. I even liked the red stripe in her hair.

I heard a noise in the hall and watched Stanley and Randall through the glass insert in the door. Stanley waved his arms as he spoke, the rumble of his voice loud but unintelligible.

I wondered what they were saying.

And I wondered what would happen to Summer.

CHAPTER 17

After what seemed like an eternity but was probably less than thirty minutes, Randall ambled into the room, his expression stern. He positioned himself between the desk and Summer, and looked at her grimly. "I've decided to give you a break. That's if you're willing to go along with what we propose."

Summer sat with her arms folded across her chest. She'd recouped her strength.

Randall slapped a folder on the desk, opened it and handed me a copy which I skimmed quickly.

"If you agree to the terms of this contract, you'll be free to go home with your aunt. If not…"

He didn't finish the sentence but the threat was obvious. He'd take her into custody.

Summer didn't blink. "You mean it?"

"Just sign this, and you can go home with your aunt."

"That's it?"

"This is not a get out of jail free card. By signing the paper, you agree to some stipulations."

She rolled her eyes. "I knew there was a catch. There's always a catch."

"Stop being so cynical," I said, losing my temper.

Randall's mustache twitched. "There's a counselor who meets at the Gray Library three times a week with a group of teenagers. He listens to what they have to say, and they talk and help each other."

"I don't need to talk with a bunch of losers. I already said I knew it was wrong to steal, and I'm sorry. Besides, I already meet with a therapist," Summer said.

Randall's frown deepened. "Save us both some time. If you aren't willing to do this, just say the word."

Summer paused a moment. "What other choice do I have?"

"So far you've made some pretty bad choices in your life. You're blaming everyone else but yourself. It's time you took responsibility for your actions. You have only yourself to blame for sitting in that chair right now. Not me, not your aunt, not your mother."

Summer stared at him, her sullen expression in place.

"If it weren't for your aunt, I wouldn't even try, but she seems to think that under your punk exterior, there's a sweet girl. Personally, I don't see it. You're probably nothing but trouble."

For a moment I disliked him, hated that he spoke so harshly to Summer. Hated that I felt like a failure for not being able to get through to her.

"You'll never amount to anything as long as you

hide behind that poor-me attitude. 'I steal because my stomach's empty.' That's a bunch of bullshit, and you know it. You aren't the only kid who's had a rough life, but not everyone hides behind excuses like you do. Try working for what you want instead of stealing."

Eyes narrowing, Summer leaned forward. "You think you got me all figured out."

"Prove me wrong," he said, pushing the file closer to her.

"I'll sign your crappy piece of paper." She scribbled her name, the handwriting barely legible.

A fleeting grin crossed Randall's face, and I realized he'd baited her. I knew that despite what he'd said, he cared a great deal.

My anger toward him vanished.

Once we returned to my house, Summer darted up the stairs and slammed the door.

Vi greeted me with a weary smile. "I'm glad you're finally home. I've been worried sick about you."

As I filled her in on what had happened, I hung up my coat in the hall closet.

Vi fidgeted with the fringe on the afghan over the back of the couch. "Let's sit, dear. I have something I need to discuss with you."

An apprehensive shiver dashed down my spine as I lowered myself onto the couch and waited to hear what she had to say.

"Summer's on a destructive path," Vi said, her voice low. "I fear you won't be able to help her. I know I can't do anything for her. I've never felt this helpless. And I certainly don't want to be responsible for her again. What if she'd been hurt? I could never live with the guilt. I hate to add to your problems, but I can't continue to watch Summer while you work. I don't mind coming over in the evenings while you're here to help with her schoolwork." She glanced across the room at Summer's picture on the mantel. "That eight-year-old child no longer exists. I'm sorry. I know I'm letting you down. But I can't bear the stress of being here alone with her. There's nothing to keep Summer from taking off again."

I certainly understood her point. But that didn't prevent panic from sweeping through me. What would I do now? How could I find someone to care for Summer on such short notice? Carrie worked three days a week so that wasn't an option. "I understand," I said, wondering how I'd manage. "I appreciate all you've done."

"I only wish I could have done more."

Shortly after Vi left, a cruiser pulled into my driveway. Randall Myers climbed out and started toward the door.

"I want to thank you for helping out Summer," I said as he neared.

When he smiled, his mustache dipped over his lower

lip, drawing my attention to his strong chin. "Maybe you should wait to thank me. If Summer slacks off, I won't go easy on her."

"I know that."

"I wonder if you do."

Strange comment. "Are you here to speak to her?"

"No, I wanted to talk to you a bit more about the contract Summer signed and what to expect from the program."

"Would you like a cup of tea, coffee or something cold to drink?"

"A cup of black coffee would be great."

He followed me into the kitchen, and I poured water into the coffeemaker and sat down. He pulled a chair away from the table, swung it around and straddled it. "I hope you don't mind my coming over here tonight, but since your niece won't be in Maine long, I figured there was no time to waste. We need to move quickly."

We.

A small word that meant so much.

I had an ally, someone who understood, someone willing to help Summer. I filled our cups and put a bag of Oreo cookies between us on the table. "Why are you so interested in helping Summer?"

A frown tugged at the corner of his mouth. "While on the force, I've seen too many throwaway kids. If I can help out a few, then I feel as though I'm making a difference."

I took a sip of coffee. My fingers absorbed the warmth from the mug.

He crossed his arms over the back of the chair. Strong masculine hands, fingers with knuckles dusted with blond hair wrapped around the rungs of the chair.

"Until last year, I worked with DARE, the Drug Abuse Resistance Education program, in the public schools educating the students about the dangers of becoming involved with drugs. But I wanted to do more, so I spoke to my chief about starting a new program aimed at helping teens in trouble. Some have already experimented with drugs. Others have parents with chemical dependency. I got the go-ahead, filled out a bunch of paperwork and received a grant from the state. I named the program TNT. Fitting because the group can at times be explosive," he said with a laugh I liked. "Teens Networking with Teens has had success getting through to teenagers otherwise lost in society. Kids that age are more likely to believe what their peers tell them. I'm hoping that Summer will open up and share what she's been through with these kids. She has a lot to gain from them, and them from her."

I took a cookie and set it down on a napkin next to my cup. "Summer won't speak to her therapist so she may refuse to talk to this group, too."

"Our counselor, Greg, has a great way with kids. Maybe because he looks like one of them. I'll introduce you when you drop off Summer tomorrow night."

"I hope this works. She's running out of time."

He lifted his mug. Deep blue eyes peered above the rim. He wasn't handsome like Tony, but his rugged good looks could not be ignored.

Anyway, his appearance made no difference. I wasn't in the market for another man.

I might never be again.

Yet as I looked into his eyes, my heart fluttered.

Was his mustache soft or bristly?

Don't go there. Concentrate on Summer, not mustaches.

"How did you persuade Stanley not to file charges?"

He unscrewed an Oreo and ate the filling. "It didn't take much persuading. Stanley comes across tough, but under all that bluster is an old softie. On my way over to the store, I called Greg to see if there was room for one more teenager in the TNT program. I pointed out to Stan what a wonderful opportunity this would be for Summer. He only hesitated a moment before agreeing to drop the charges."

The shock must have shown on my face because Randall said, "You didn't expect that."

I toyed with the cookie on my napkin. "I'd thought Stan was a cold-hearted man."

"The guy has a heart of gold and will do anything for a teen in trouble."

"I'd have never guessed…"

"Stan's daughter, Sara, went through a rough time with the law, and with the help of the TNT program, she was able to turn her life around. Stan believes in second chances. I do, too."

"Keeping the program going sounds very time-consuming. What's in it for you?"

"I want to make a difference."

"I'm impressed."

"Don't be." For a moment his eyes clouded with misery. "I'm doing this for a purely selfish reason. Six years ago my younger sister, Caitlin, died of an overdose. Maybe if I hadn't been so absorbed in my own life, I would have seen she needed my help. Doing this helps me to live with myself." He glanced away a moment, and when he looked at me again, the haunted look had disappeared. "It's too late for Caitlin, but it's not too late for lots of other kids. So I'm doing my damnedest to help every child who'll let me, and that includes Summer. Plus, I was impressed when she said she'd never take drugs. She was adamant. I want the other kids to hear her say that."

I wasn't sure how I felt about him using Summer to achieve his goals. "I thought the point of signing Summer into the program was to help her."

"Definitely. But by talking to other teenagers, everyone comes away ahead of the game. While Summer is in this program, it's important for you to be firm and not let her get away with anything. You'll need to stop treating her like a little child and expect her to make adult decisions."

"But she's only thirteen."

He polished off two more cookies and nodded. "She's street smart and much older than her chronological age. She's had to grow up quickly. Too quickly. Plus, if her mother starts doing drugs again, she needs to be prepared to take care of herself. For TNT to work, we need to be on the same team. No babying her. You can't show her your soft side."

"What's wrong with being compassionate?"

"Summer knows she can play you, and she'll use that to her advantage. Like she did earlier today. According to Stanley, she didn't shed one tear until you showed up."

"She was upset and frightened," I said, back in my defensive mode.

"She was tugging at your emotions, and doing a damn good job of it, too. But I'm convinced beneath that thick shell she's built around herself is a good kid."

"What makes you say that? You don't know her like I do. And at times, I wonder if I know her at all."

"It was idiotic of her to try to rip off Stanley, but her intentions—to help you out—were on the right track. She obviously cares for you, and a truly bad kid wouldn't care about anyone but herself."

I really liked this man.

His mouth curved into a wide smile. "I saw the way you looked at her when she played the 'I need to steal for food' sympathy card."

"I was shocked."

"And it showed. She said that to get to you."

"You really think so?"

"I know so. Even if she were starving, there are better ways to get food than stealing it. Go to a soup kitchen, or a church, go to social services."

"Maybe she didn't know that."

"Maybe not, but she didn't steal a jar of peanut butter, a loaf of bread and some broccoli. Back in L.A., she and her friends were picked up for breaking and entering. They stole electronics and jewelry. Because Summer didn't have any prior record, she was let go."

That destroyed my image of a starving child running off with a piece of fruit. I rose to my feet and took both cups to the sink and rinsed them.

As Randall stood, I heard the crackle of leather. "At times, stealing can seem like an easy solution, but it's not. Summer needs to find alternative methods to fulfill her needs."

Even with my back to him, I felt his presence. I turned and managed a smile. "I'll do whatever it takes to help her."

He stepped closer and shook my hand.

"Welcome aboard, partner."

Early the next day I called my assistant and told her I wouldn't be in. I left a message for my supervisor, Edith Wilcox, to call me.

A while later the phone rang.

"Edith, I had wanted to come in to talk to you in person, but it's not possible. I know this is bad timing, but I need to take a leave of absence."

An uneasy silence ensued. "We're already way behind, and the end-of-the-year crunch is coming up fast. I really need you to be here."

"I'm sorry, but until my niece goes home…"

"How long will you be gone?"

"Three weeks. Once Summer leaves, I'll be back, ready to throw myself into the job." A thought struck that might save my job. "If you're willing, I can work from home after Summer goes to bed."

"We'll give it a try and see what happens."

"You won't regret this."

"Keep in mind, there are other qualified women vying for your position. You're still on probation. This leave of absence won't look good on your record."

That evening I knocked on Summer's door. "Are you almost ready?"

"I don't wanna go."

I swung the door open and marched across the room. She sat on the bed, arms folded, stubborn chin raised.

"You're going to this meeting or you're going to jail. You decide."

She leaned over and tied her black boots. "I said I

was sorry and won't do it again. What more do you want from me?"

"I want you to get up this instant. Walk out that door and plant your butt in my car. I want you to do whatever I tell you, and if you refuse to talk to that group of teenagers and the therapist, you won't be at basketball tryouts tomorrow night."

"You're just like the rest of them, always ordering me around."

"If you did what you were supposed to on your own, I wouldn't have to order you around."

"Whatever happened to the sweet, soft-spoken aunt I remember?"

"She's gone. Just like that sweet eight-year-old I remember."

CHAPTER 18

When we arrived at the library, Randall Myers was speaking to a stocky man with long hair pulled back in a ponytail. The man wore a faded T-shirt with the sleeves ripped off and torn jeans. Vine tattoos ringed his muscular arms.

As we neared, Randall smiled and waved us over. "Summer, I'm glad you made it."

"Yeah, right, like I had a choice."

"This is Greg Peters, your counselor."

"Glad to meet you," she said, with a bite-me smirk.

Greg shook Summer's hand. As he started to tell her about the rest of the gang, his brown eyes filled with excitement. "It's a good group. You'll soon feel right at home."

Summer threw him an incredulous look. "Whatever."

Undaunted, Greg continued, "They're a great bunch of kids, and if you give them half a chance, you'll grow to like them."

"I gotta love the losers," she said. "Or I don't get to play basketball."

I met her stony gaze. "That's a fact so you better keep that in mind."

When I looked up, an approving grin flitted across Randall's face. For a moment I remembered how he'd taken my hand and called me partner, how my fingers had tingled under his touch.

We were a team. A team of three, because I sensed that Greg also wanted Summer to succeed.

It felt good to know that someone else cared what happened to her.

"Wait for me. I'll be back in a sec," Randall said, a warm smile directed at me.

Randall took Summer's arm, but she promptly shrugged him off. "Let me show you around and introduce you to the others." He led the way down the stairs.

After sending me an anguished look, Summer followed.

Summer wore black army boots, baggy jeans with holes in the knees and butt, and a camouflage army jacket over a bright pink top with metallic hearts across her chest. She'd spiked the top of her hair, and allowed soft wisps to cover her ears. She wore a thick leather band with metal prongs on her right wrist along with the charm bracelet.

She hadn't worn the bracelet since the day I'd given it to her. And because she'd been upset with me earlier, I considered the bracelet a good sign—an omen for a possible loving relationship between us. Summer talked tough, but there was an endearing side to her that few people saw.

Greg started down the steps and glanced over his shoulder. "Don't look so worried. She's in good hands."

As I stood there, clenching my fingers, I hoped this would be a turning point for my niece.

Randall returned a few minutes later. "Would you like to go somewhere for a cup of coffee?"

"I'm staying right here in case Summer decides to leave."

"Greg won't let that happen. Once the teens are downstairs, they must stay for the entire meeting. It's a rule."

I groaned. "In case you haven't noticed, Summer doesn't listen to rules."

"Greg positions his chair right in front of the stairway. No one leaves early unless they go through him. Summer may be stubborn, but she's a tiny thing. Brute force won't work for her."

"I'm sure you're right, Randall, but I can't leave. If I did, I'd worry the entire time."

"Annie, my friends call me Randy. Randall sounds too formal, and I'm an easygoing kind of guy."

"Okay, Randy." I liked his name, and even more, the way he said mine.

He grinned. "You stand guard right here, and I'll go

buy us a couple cups of coffee at Dunkin' Donuts and be right back. Then I'll park in front so we can watch the door from inside my cruiser."

Fascinated by his mustache and how it moved when he spoke, I lost myself for a moment. Fortunately, when he turned and walked out the door, I returned to my senses.

Right now, I needed to focus on Summer. There wasn't time to become involved with another man.

The next night, Mallory decided to join me and watch Summer's coed basketball practice. Less than a dozen parents sat at a distance chatting among themselves.

"Go, girl," Mallory shouted, jumping up from her seat. "Did you see that? Summer stole the ball away from that tall, geeky-looking guy. She's awesome."

"Of course I saw that. Didn't you hear me holler?" I asked, sitting back down.

"You look exhausted."

"I didn't get to bed until four. I'm trying to keep up with my work."

"You look like you're about ready to fall over. You need to take better care of yourself."

"Once Summer goes back home, I'll get back to my normal schedule."

"You're doing a great job with her."

I thought so, but it was nice to hear the words. "Thanks."

Mallory examined one of her fingernails. "Darn, look at that. I've chipped another nail."

I flashed a quick glance at the damage. As I looked back at the court, I saw Summer making another basket. "Way to go, Summer!"

Mallory grabbed a nail file from her purse. "Is there anything new with Summer?"

"I told her tonight that she doesn't have to return to the other therapist. She said that was cool, so at the moment she's happy with me. I asked her what went on in her group session last night. 'Stuff' was her reply."

"Why not phone Greg and ask him what went on?"

"I already tried that. According to Greg, whatever happens in the group stays with the group. Everything that's said is confidential. If he loses their trust, the kids will stop opening up to him. So I'm left in the dark."

"That's too bad."

"I just hope these sessions help her."

She tucked her nail file into her pocket. "How's her reading coming along?"

I bit down on my lower lip. "Vi's still upset with her for running off, and it shows. Vi can be a very generous lady, but when she's unhappy it's written all over her face. Earlier today, Vi come over to tutor Summer. Before she left, I offered to take over the lessons. She instantly agreed, saying she'd make up the lesson plans and help me any way she could."

"That's a shame. However, as you know, I've always

considered Vi a royal pain in the butt. What you see in that woman is beyond me."

"She's always been there for me. And she tried to help with Summer, but she no longer wants to be responsible for her care. I don't blame her."

"I'd help if I could, but we both know my grammar skills aren't that great."

"Actually I'm looking forward to spending more time with Summer. I hope we'll grow closer. And I feel better keeping Vi and Summer apart. I don't want my niece thinking Vi doesn't like her."

"Well, she doesn't."

I covered my mouth and yawned. "The feelings between Vi and Summer are mutual. The less time they spend together, the better. When those two are in the same room, you can feel the tension."

"Fortunately, it's for only a few weeks." Mallory dug a pack of Tic Tacs from her purse.

I held out my hand so she'd tap a few into my palm. "Two weeks and five days, not that I'm counting."

She popped one into her mouth. "If it were me, I'd have the time figured out to the minute. Speaking of that, have you heard from your sister?"

"Dana called this morning. She sounded really excited about her rehab program and is convinced it'll change her life forever. She's certain she's through with drugs, and I'm starting to believe her."

"That's great."

"Yet I still worry she might screw up."

"Dana's older, and maybe wiser. This time might do the trick."

"I'm hoping it does. I'm trying to think only good thoughts about her rehab, but…it's easy to remember the other times she failed."

"Then only focus on the present."

"I'm trying." But as hard as I tried, it was impossible not to wonder whether Dana still considered rehab a hiatus from motherhood. Did she miss Summer? And if so, why didn't she mention her when she called? Why was I the one to suggest she speak to her daughter?

Mallory put the candy between us. "John has a buddy who's looking to meet someone nice."

Her questioning gaze pierced right through me. "You're not trying to set me up with him."

"Why not?"

"No way."

"It would be fun. We could double date."

"I'm done with men for a while. Plus, there's Summer to consider. I need to be with her as much as possible. Why don't you ask Carrie?"

Mallory made a face. "I would, but this guy isn't into kids."

"That's too bad. I know how much she'd like to get married."

"That's the problem. If the guy isn't looking for a serious relationship, she isn't interested."

"She has her boys to consider."

"But what's wrong with having a little fun? She's the one missing out."

"Maybe, but if the man isn't what she's looking for, why waste time?"

"Hmmm," she said, a faraway look in her eyes. "I've been asking myself the same thing. About John."

"I thought you were breaking up with him."

"I was going to, but...it isn't easy."

"I'd think you'd be an expert by now."

"You'd think so, wouldn't you, but this time, it's a bit more complicated."

"Meaning?"

"I let him hang around too long. Now I'm hooked."

"Leave it to you to say hooked instead of what you really mean."

She wagged her finger. But I saw the truth.

"Don't say it. Or I'll break out in hives. You know I have a severe allergy to the *L* word."

I laughed along with her.

"John isn't satisfied with the way things are," Mallory said. "He wants more. He's ruined everything. Why couldn't he have left well enough alone?"

"Maybe because he cares a lot about you."

Frowning, Mallory stared at the basketball court and said nothing for a minute. Summer sat on the sidelines beside other players. From here she looked like a happy teenager as she spoke to the guy sitting next to her.

A humorless chuckle bubbled past Malloy's throat. "John wants to marry me and have babies."

"Is that so bad?" I pictured an infant in its crib, and my heart lurched. "Why are you so afraid of commitment?"

She lifted pain-filled eyes. "You of all people should understand."

When I realized what she meant, a familiar hollow ache expanded inside. "Just because Tony turned out to be a louse, doesn't mean all men are jerks."

Mallory inclined her head and waited a moment.

"Okay, Paul, too, but some of the blame is mine, for not seeing what they were like."

"There are an awful lot of happy women walking around blindly, who think they're married to the perfect man. Then when they least expect it, someone else comes along. And *kaboom*, their little world blows apart."

Mallory wasn't one to mince words, and unlike Carrie who thought good things about everyone, including Tony, I appreciated that Mallory saw all relationships as doomed.

"Not everyone's marriage falls apart," I said.

"When a marriage lasts, it's probably because there's a stubborn woman willing to overlook hubby's transgressions. My father was a philanderer, and so were my uncles. Why my mother put up with his cheating, I'll never understand. But there's no way in hell I'm going to follow in her footsteps."

Mallory had never spoken to Carrie or me about her parents. For that matter, we knew little about her past. The few times we'd asked questions, she'd quickly changed the subject. "I'm sorry to hear that."

"Don't be. My parents' marriage and parenting skills served as excellent bad examples. I learned my lessons well, then I packed my bags and didn't look back."

"How long has it been since you went home?"

"Not long enough," she said, anguish echoing in her tone. "Face it, men are a low life form, put on Earth to propagate the world. Since I don't intend to have kids, I'm certainly not going to complicate my life by getting married. Unfortunately, I've broken the biggest commandment of them all." She hesitated a moment, her expression clouding. "I've fallen in love with the guy."

She'd said love. For a moment I just stared at her. Something inside me wrenched. "If you love him, you can't send him away."

"He loves me, too."

I placed my hands over hers. "You should be happy. Go for it. Maybe it'll work out."

"Not a chance. He wants the entire package, a small three-bedroom cape, a wife and kids. I'm too old to have children."

"You're only thirty-nine."

"I'll be forty in two months."

"Lots of older women have babies."

She shook her head, glanced down and tapped her

fingernails on the wooden bleacher between us. "I'm not ready to take such a big step. I'll never be ready. John deserves to have children of his own. That won't happen if he stays with me."

"Maybe he loves you enough to forgo having children."

"He's an only child, and he tells me his mother can't wait to have grandchildren. That said, he claims he doesn't want to lose me, and that he'll do anything including give up his chances for a family if I'll marry him."

"Well, there you go. Problem solved."

"In years to come, he'll think back to the sacrifice he's made, and he'll hate me. I know what I need to do. For his sake."

CHAPTER 19

The following morning I made pancakes for breakfast. When Summer was done eating, I handed her a notebook and explained what I had in mind.

"Vi isn't coming over to tutor you today."

Summer punched the air victoriously.

I knew Vi wasn't disappointed either. "I thought I'd help you with your reading, and at the same time, we'll have a little fun."

Looking skeptical, Summer shrugged. "Yeah, right, like doing schoolwork is ever going to be fun." She thumbed through the empty notebook. "What's this for?"

"I decided it's time you learned to read words that mean something to you." I handed her a short story I'd typed earlier. "Let's sit down and read this. Then we're off to the mall to do some shopping and learn more words."

Summer rolled her eyes. "This is boring." She dropped down onto a kitchen chair and glanced at the paper. "Why are some of the words in yellow?"

"I highlighted the key word, those that I thought

would be important to a future basketball star. Instead of learning random words, you're going to read those that make a difference in your life."

She started to read, "Summer…" She pointed to the first highlighted word. "This is too hard. I can't do it."

I sat beside her. "I don't expect you to know this right away, but with a bit of effort, you'll soon recognize these words, and we'll add others. We're going to read this together. Then later, you'll spend a bit of time writing each word down three times, soon you'll know them. That word is 'caught.' Summer caught the rebound." I waited for her to continue.

"Last night," she read, looking pleased. "I didn't think you knew about rebounds."

"I looked up the information online. So continue from there," I said, pointing to the next sentence.

"Summer…"

"Stole…"

"The ball from…"

"A tall geek."

We both laughed. "That was Mallory's observation," I explained.

We worked on her lesson for another thirty minutes. Then we went into the living room, and she helped me tape labels to the furniture. When we were done, everything in the room had a tag in bold lettering.

"In three days, I'm going to remove these labels and

expect you to write down the words for each one. Soon you'll be able to read hundreds of words. And you'll be able to attend any school you want because your grades will be good. In time maybe you'll play college ball, and I'll be sitting in the stands, cheering you on."

"Give me a break. I'm never ever gonna be able to go to college."

"Why not?"

"Because…"

"Don't you dare say it," I warned her.

"Well, it's true."

"You're wrong, and I'm determined to prove it to you."

"Anyway, I could never afford to go to college."

"You might be able to get a basketball scholarship, and I'll help pay for your tuition."

"You'd do that for me?"

"You bet I would. Aim high, Summer. I have faith in you."

Looking pleased but doubtful, she pointed to the card on the television. "That word would be a lot easier if you'd just written TV."

I gave her arm an affectionate squeeze. "But the point to this exercise is to challenge you. Now, grab your coat. We're going on a word hunt, shopping spree." I shoved several note cards into her hand. "Whichever words you can read, I'll buy that item for you."

She stared at the first word. "Can…dy. It says candy. I did it."

"Yes, you did. You win the prize. I'll buy whatever kind of candy you want."

"What's the catch?"

"You'll have to add the name of the candy to your list," I said, with a satisfied grin.

"Then I want M&M's. That's easy to spell."

"You're a clever kid. Now can you read any of the other cards?"

She shuffled through a few before she stopped at a short simple word I'd planted there, hoping she'd recognize it.

"Ohmygod. It says cat! Do you mean a real cat?"

"The kind that goes meow," I said, smiling. "Would you like to get a kitten?"

"Yes, more than anything. It's a good thing you didn't write the word *kitten* or I'd have never figured it out."

That's what I'd thought. "In that case, you'll have to add kitten to your list."

"Where are we going for a kitten? What if there aren't any kittens? Oh my gosh, I bet they're all out of kittens."

"I've already called the shelter. They have several to pick from."

"C-A-T. This just might work out," she said, grabbing her jacket. As she darted out the door, there was a new look in her eyes.

Hope.

Summer was starting to believe in herself.

* * *

We returned a few hours later. We'd had a productive day. Summer seemed thrilled with her reading progress as she carried the cardboard box with vented holes into the living room.

When she opened the lid, a yellow tiger kitten leaped out, scampered across the room and dashed back again.

"What are you going to name him?"

"I don't know. I've never had a pet before," she said, her eyes bright. "I want a really special name." She tapped her fingers along the floor and the kitten leaped for her hand, climbed up her jacket sleeve, and sat on her shoulder.

She giggled. "His whiskers tickle my neck. Isn't he a riot?"

"He's cute."

"Maybe I'll call him Speedy, or Riot, or gee… I'll need to think about it." Worry twisted her features into a frown. "What if my mom won't let me keep him?"

"I've already spoken to her, and she said it was all right."

"But what if she changes her mind and decides I can't take him home with me?"

She expected Dana to disappoint her—again.

"Then he'll stay here with me, and you'll be able to visit him often."

"I guess." She took the kitten down from her shoulder and threw a tiny ball we'd bought across the floor.

The kitten ran after the toy, grabbed it and skidded to a stop, the ball in his mouth. "I'm going to name him Mr. T, short for Mr. Trouble, because he's going to get into things he shouldn't. Like me," she said, with another laugh.

As the tiny animal ran circles around us, Summer leaned in close and kissed my cheek. "Thanks, this is the best present anyone's ever given me."

In that instant, I knew I'd found the sweet girl I remembered. I figured everything was going to be all right.

One week later, Summer had made amazing progress. She knew how to spell the words for every piece of furniture in the living room and kitchen. Everywhere she went inside the house so did Mr. T. When she ate breakfast, he'd play at her feet. When she worked on her lessons, he'd sometimes sit on her lap and swipe at her pencil. Other times, he'd scoot onto the table and we'd shoo him off. When she slept, he curled in a ball under the blankets next to her.

"Listen to this," Summer said, showing me a note she'd written. "Mom, I hope you are OK. Annie is nice. I am being good. I am good at basketball and sort of good at reading. I have a kitten. He is nice. He is Mr. T. I miss you. Love, Summer."

"That's wonderful," I said, the lump in my throat swelling.

"It's not a big deal. I just looked up the words on my cards and copied the ones I wanted."

"It *is* a big deal. You knew which words to use. Which means you read them."

"I didn't really read them. I memorized them."

"Same difference," I said, grinning. "Soon you'll be able to read everything, the newspaper, novels."

"This reading crap isn't as hard as I expected it to be."

"That's because you're smart."

She shrugged. "I'm not as dumb as I thought I was."

"Is this your way of agreeing with me?"

"Yeah, I guess so."

Later that week at basketball practice, I was watching Summer on the court when Randy arrived.

"Hey, what are you doing here?" I asked.

"I promised Summer I'd come watch her play," he said, taking off his jacket and sitting beside me.

Disappointment came out of nowhere, jolted me when I realized I wanted him to be there for me, too.

Ridiculous.

It was the first time I'd seen him out of uniform, and the transformation was truly amazing. He wore a leather jacket, dark slacks, a deep blue sweater that accented his eyes, eyes that for a moment caught me off guard, held my gaze a few seconds longer than necessary.

Heat rose to my face.

Foolish widow.

You don't even want to become involved with any man.

So why did Randy steal into my thoughts when I least expected? The other night I'd even dreamed about him. I'd awakened feeling warm inside.

Get a grip.

Randy smiled. "Greg said to tell you Summer's making good progress. I'd like her to speak to the kids in the DARE program and explain what she's been through so they can hear firsthand what harm drugs can do."

"Summer would never agree to do that."

"She already has."

"Are you serious?" I asked, thinking I'd heard wrong.

"I would never joke about anything this important. Summer's connected with Greg's group. They've listened to her stories in awe. And she's learned a lot from them, too. It's given her confidence in herself."

"If Summer wants to speak to the DARE group, she certainly has my support."

"You're the greatest," he said, which hiked my temperature a few degrees. "Summer thinks the world of you. And I happen to think she's right."

His compliment took me off guard. I blushed like a schoolgirl. "Thanks."

The following week, I sat in the Gray gym next to Carrie and Mallory while Officer Randall Myers handed out DARE T-shirts to the children.

Summer stood by the door waiting for his introduction. She threw me a helpless look. She was nervous, but not as nervous as I was. I could barely sit still. My pulse pounded in my ears.

I looked forward to leaving, when Summer would be done speaking. It wasn't that I didn't have confidence in her. But I wasn't used to sitting in a group while my child performed or talked. Technically, she wasn't really mine, but she was as close as I'd ever come to having a daughter of my own.

Randy waved for Summer to join him. "We have a special guest here this evening. Her name is Summer. She'll be going back to Los Angeles next week, but she wanted to tell you what drugs did to her life, in hopes that if one of you is tempted, you'll remember what she said and shout, 'No way.'"

Summer walked into the center of the gym and stood next to Randy.

She looked small but in control.

Unlike me, trembling in my seat.

"My name is Summer, and I wouldn't do drugs if someone paid me a bunch of money. I've done lots of stupid things, but I would never take a puff on a joint. Some of you have probably already smoked weed, and you don't think it's a big thing. Well, you're wrong...."

I was impressed with the strength in her voice. She commanded the attention of her audience. And she got it.

Pride soared through me.

Carrie gently elbowed my ribs. "I can't believe how good she is."

Mallory added, "She could be a motivational speaker. Summer's changed a lot since I first met her at DiMillo's."

"She's really something special," I said, for a moment smiling at Randy when he glanced at me.

Mallory bent close to my ear. "Who's the hottie?"

"That's Officer Randall Myers, the policeman I told you about."

"You didn't mention that he is gorgeous."

"I hadn't noticed."

"Liar." Mallory scrutinized me for a moment. "You look terrible."

"I worked until three this morning."

"How long do you think you can keep that up?"

"I'm fine, really."

Holding the microphone near her chin, Summer cleared her throat. "My mother started out smoking pot, then she tried a bunch of other stuff. She lost lots of jobs, and there were times when we had no electricity or water because she had no money to pay the bills. Once we even camped out in an alley for a few days because we got thrown out of our apartment. At first, I thought it was kinda cool, but then it started to rain and we all got soaked. I still remember how I couldn't stop shivering. Some of you are sitting there thinking you're too smart to get hooked. Well…you're wrong. I came home one day and found my mom on the floor. Her arms were at a weird angle, and she had a strange expression on her face. I called her name, but she didn't move. When I put my finger under her nose…" Summer's voice faltered, and a girl in the front row wiped her eyes. "I thought she was dead."

I shuddered at the image that sprang into my mind. Of Summer, afraid and alone when she saw Dana, unconscious.

"If help hadn't arrived when it did, my mom would have died. But she's going to be okay."

The children in the room heaved a collective sigh.

Summer paused. "My mom's finally smartened up. She's in rehab, and she's doing great. She's coming home soon, and I can't wait to see her again."

Carrie dabbed at the tears in the corners of her eyes. "I don't know how you two can sit there without crying. This is so sad."

Mallory tapped a long fingernail on her purse. "Summer is a talented speaker. She could sell tap water to Poland Springs bottling."

"Anyway," Summer said. "I want to say one more thing, and then I'll shut up. Because my mother was spaced out a lot, I did my own thing. I didn't have a curfew, had no one to order me around. Which I thought was kinda cool, but now I know it's not cool at all. I got in a lot of trouble at school and with the police. I could blame my mom, but I won't. I'm responsible for my actions. You're responsible for the dumb decisions you make, too. And I hope if any of you are thinking of trying drugs that you'll smarten up before it's too late. You could end up in rehab like my mom. Or you could end up dead."

Summer handed the microphone to Randy, and as the parents and children in the audience clapped, she walked across the room and sat next to me.

I was the proudest woman in the room.

CHAPTER 20

Summer and I were working on her reading the next morning when the doorbell chimed. She went to answer the door and returned with a long-stemmed rose and a brightly wrapped box.

She handed me the card. "It's from Randy and the kids I spoke to last night. No one's ever given me a flower."

From the first time I'd met Randy, I'd thought he was special. I'd been right. "What's in the box?"

She removed the bow, tugged at the ribbon, and opened the lid. "It's a basketball. Look at all the names on it," she said, taking it out of the box. "'You blew everyone away, Randy. You Rock, Jill. You're the best!, Seth.' Thanks to you, I can read most of the words," she said, looking up, her voice filled with gratitude.

Maybe it was fatigue from trying to keep up with only a few hours of sleep each night, or maybe it was knowing that soon Summer would leave and I wouldn't see her every day, but I felt incredibly emotional. Happy, sad, bittersweet, all at once.

Don't cry. Get a hold of yourself.

Above Randy's name in a masculine scrawl, he'd written, "Summer, you're my heroine." My resolve crumbling, I dashed away a tear. "This is a wonderful gift."

"It's awesome. I can't wait to show it to my mom. Only a few more days, and she'll be here."

I nodded and tried to ignore the apprehensive shiver that slid down my spine. I hadn't heard from Dana in a few days, and as the date of her arrival drew nearer, I'd begun to realize how much I'd miss my niece.

As if summoned by my thoughts, the phone rang. Summer picked it up. "Hey, Mom, you won't believe what I just got. A real rose and a basketball. You shoulda heard me at the DARE gathering last night. I really rocked."

I waited for a pause and then gestured. "When you're through, I want to speak to Dana."

She smiled and nodded. "Can we stay at Annie's until Tuesday? I wanna be in the first basketball game next Monday so you can see me play."

I held my breath.

Summer laughed. "That's cool. I'm sure Annie won't mind having us here for a while."

She shot a questioning glance at me and I said, "Of course not."

Exhilaration bubbled up inside me. Though I'd miss Summer, more than anything, I wanted her to be happy.

"Have you got your ticket yet?"

Once more I held my breath.

"Shouldn't you have done that by now?" Summer asked and paused. "I guess that makes sense. So we aren't going to rent a car and drive back?" Summer leaned against the kitchen counter. "Oh, I see. What did you think of the note I sent you? I wrote it all by myself."

The smile slipped from her face. "It's no big deal. It was only a crummy few words on a piece of paper."

Not a big deal!

That note was a symbol of all she'd accomplished.

My insides clenched with anger. Dana should be encouraging Summer.

"Okay, me too. Annie wants to talk to you." Summer handed me the phone and left the room.

I schooled my tone. "Hi, Dana, when will you be flying out?"

"I'm not sure. As I already told Summer, cash is a bit tight so I'm going to have to take the red-eye. And even then, I don't know how I'm going to swing it. I might have to work at a fast-food joint for a couple weeks."

Intense dislike flooded through me. "You can't disappoint Summer again. She's been counting down the days and the hours."

Guilt nudged me. Sisters were supposed to be close, share secrets, enjoy spending time together.

Love each other.

"You can't get blood from a stone or money from a bush."

"Why didn't you mention this sooner?"

Summer came into the kitchen for a glass of water. And maybe to listen to the conversation.

"I just figured it out. Until now, I've had to concentrate on getting clean. I've made remarkable progress. Instead of trying to lay a guilt trip on me, you should be congratulating me. You don't have any idea what I've been through."

"I'm sure it was rough."

"It was hell."

Though I was sympathetic, if Summer were not in the room, I'd have pointed out the separation had been rough on her, too. And where Dana had chosen to do drugs, Summer was an innocent casualty of my sister's bad judgment. "I'll check on the flight schedule and get back to you. It's very important you get here in time for the game."

"What game?"

Damn. Didn't she listen to what Summer was telling her? "Summer's a whiz at basketball. You'll be impressed when you see her play. The first big game is on Monday evening. I'll try to book your flight for Saturday."

Summer glanced at me, smiling.

"Oh yeah, she did mention something about that."

It's all Summer had talked about. How could she not

remember? "I'll charge the plane ticket on my card, and you can repay me later."

"Yeah, I'll do that."

If broken promises were dollars, Dana would be rich. "Call me tomorrow night and I'll give you the information for your flight."

Summer walked past and leaned into the phone. "See you soon, Mom. Can't wait." She pushed the door open and left the room, clutching her rose and her basketball.

"I'd better be going. I don't want to be late for the last group meeting," Dana said.

"Before you hang up, there's something I want to discuss with you."

"Uh-oh, what have I done now?"

"You need to be more attentive to Summer's needs. You can't go through life ignoring your own daughter."

"I give her plenty of attention," she replied, sounding aggravated.

"I'm sure you try, but you need to try harder. For instance, whatever happened to that note she sent you?"

"You don't know what it's like here. It's all I can do to focus on myself."

"She wrote that note for you all by herself. It meant a lot to her, and she was proud of what she'd accomplished. Do you know Summer couldn't even read when she first arrived?"

"She was getting by fine in school, that is when she went."

"And whose fault is that?"

"I can't force her to attend school if she doesn't want to. That kid has a mind of her own."

You aren't doing enough. I blew out a calming breath and tried to keep my tone level. "I know that, but you need to be firm with her. Force her to go to school. Bring her there each day and pick her up if you have to. When she's grown and looks back on what you've done, she'll understand, and she'll love you for it."

"Look, I'm doing my best here. Stop lecturing me. You don't know what it's like raising a kid. So don't go preaching like you just got crowned mother of the year."

The next evening, I sat in the bleachers with my briefcase by my side, my laptop on my knees, trying to pay attention to the game and at the same time, finish a report for Edith.

I was aware of someone sitting down next to me, but I didn't know who it was until I heard his voice.

"You look like a career woman ready to collapse," Randy said.

Goose bumps peppered my flesh. I turned, met his deep blue eyes and lost myself for a moment. "Hey, how's it going?"

"Fine, but I'm worried about you. Summer mentioned how hard you've been working."

Their concern touched me. I hadn't expected Summer to notice. "I'm just doing a little catch-up."

"Are you sure that's all there is? You don't look as though you're feeling well."

"It's nothing that can't be cured with several more hours of sleep. And once I've completed this report, I'm through working for the bank until next Wednesday so I'll have plenty of time to rest." Another sharp pain jabbed into my right side. I counted slowly to ten. The familiar ache pulsed, subsided and disappeared, proving once again that I'd taxed my body to its limit.

"I didn't know you were coming to practice," I said.

"I won't be able to go to the first big game because I need to work, which is a damn shame. I tried to switch days but no one could take my shift." He handed me a business card with the police department's phone number on it. "I've penciled in my unlisted home phone number on the back in case you ever need to reach me."

"Thanks." After glancing at his choppy handwriting, I put the card in my jacket pocket. I couldn't fathom why I'd need to reach him. But I could easily imagine why I'd want to call: because I liked him, or just to hear the sound of his voice.

"Just because Summer is leaving, that's no reason for us to lose touch," he said, for a moment reaching over and placing his hand over mine.

A current ran through me, left me yearning for intimacy.

When he took his hand away, I released a breath.

I'd had little luck concentrating before Randy arrived, now I couldn't concentrate at all. So I put my laptop away and tried to focus on the practice instead of the slight pressure from Randy's thigh against mine.

We cheered, we shouted, we jumped up and down each time Summer made a basket or a play. During a short break, I felt my eyes close. My head jerked forward and I forced myself to stay awake. But before long, my eyelids drooped and as though I were in a fog, I felt myself slipping away.

I awoke with a start when I heard Summer's voice and realized I'd fallen asleep with my head against Randy's shoulder.

"The basketball you sent was really cool. So was the flower," she said.

"I'm glad you liked it. The kids in the DARE program were blown away by your talk."

"Gee, thanks."

Feeling rather foolish, I sat up straight. I was here to watch Summer practice, not to take a nap. "Sorry, I didn't mean to fall asleep," I said to Summer who shrugged as though it didn't matter.

"I'd like to take you two girls out for a celebration meal," Randy said, looking from Summer to me. "That's if you're up to it?"

"Of course I'm up to it. What's the occasion?"

"Summer is through with her group session, and Greg says she's been an inspiration to every kid there."

Summer rolled her eyes. "It's not as though I'm done with the group because I don't need it. It's because I'm leaving."

"That's true, but you've come a long way, kiddo," Randy said, scrubbing his knuckles over her head. "I'm really hungry so how's that for a reason? Annie, are you hungry?"

"I could eat something." In fact, I'd eaten very little in the last few days. Was I coming down with the flu? Or had my sister's impending arrival wreaked havoc with my stomach?

"Great, then that's settled," he said, looping an arm through my elbow and following Summer who'd already started down the bleachers.

On the way to Friday's, a restaurant in Portland, Summer chatted while I drove.

"I can't wait for the game. It's too bad it'll be my last. Well, not really my last game, because I plan to join another team when I get back home, but you know what I mean."

I nodded and turned right.

"It's hard to believe that next week at this time, I'll be back home. I wonder where me and mom are going to live."

I felt another twinge on my right side, confirming my pain was stress induced. "I'm sure the rehab center wouldn't release her unless she has somewhere to go."

"Anyway, I can't wait to show her my new stuff. My

flower might not look very good by then, but I'm gonna keep it forever. And there's no way I'll ever use that basketball. I plan to put it on my bureau in my bedroom. When I look at it, I'll remember my trip to Maine."

"If you'd like, tomorrow after I drop off my work at the bank, you and I will go shopping for a new charm for your bracelet."

"Cool."

Later that night after we arrived home, Mr. T greeted us at the door. Summer picked him up and scratched behind his ears. I noticed on caller ID that Dana had phoned. I regretted missing her call because I'd wanted to know her plans for after she was released.

"Good night." Summer kissed my cheek, which pleased me.

"Sleep tight," I said, and watched her walk up the stairs, cradling her kitten in her arms. As she disappeared into her room, I knew I'd miss her a lot.

She'll forever own a piece of my heart.

It also struck me that I wanted to move back into my old bedroom, the one I'd shared with Paul, and convert the bedroom I'd been using into an office.

Surprising, considering I'd never expected to be able to sleep in that room again.

Before I could question this discovery, the phone rang, and I ran to answer it.

DIANE AMOS

"Sis, did you find me a flight?"

"Yes." I'd printed out the information and put it next to the phone. I picked up the paper and read it to Dana.

"Then I'll see you Saturday around noon," she said.

"Summer is so excited. You're all she talks about. She can't wait for you to watch her basketball game. You will be staying for that?"

My right side pulsed as I held my breath.

"Yeah, I thought I'd stay and sponge a couple meals off you." Dana laughed.

And I breathed a sigh of relief. "After you get here, I'll help you with your flights heading home. I'll pay extra so Summer can take Mr. T onto the plane."

"Who the hell is Mr. T?"

My right side flared up. I gripped the phone tight and counted slowly to seven. No wonder my muscles tensed whenever I spoke to Dana.

"Mr. T is Summer's kitten. She's told you about him."

"Oh yeah, I guess I forgot."

I groaned.

"Don't go getting on my case. I've had a lot on my mind you know."

"Have you found a place for you and Summer to stay?"

When she hesitated, my right side throbbed—hard.

"I think so."

"What's that supposed to mean?"

"It means I'm all set."

"I sure hope that's true." And I knew what I had to do, for Summer's sake. "If you need a loan until you get settled, I can advance you some cash."

"Yeah, that would sure come in handy. I got some good news to share, but first you have to promise not to go ballistic."

My right side pulsed like a drum. "If it's good news, why would I get upset?"

"It's the way you react whenever I tell you anything. It's like you can't stand seeing me happy."

I sat on the couch and tried to sound patient. "Of course I want you to be happy. I want Summer to be happy."

"Good, because I haven't told anyone else, but…I'm in love."

Not again.

"When did this happen?"

"It came on suddenly. One minute he's just a guy in my rehab group, the next I'm *wowed*, and I'm feeling dizzy just looking at him."

"He's a drug addict?" I asked, my voice shrill.

"Calm down."

"Don't tell me to calm down!"

"I knew you'd freak. He's a recovered addict, like me. And he's really cute."

"I cannot believe—"

"Anyway, your speech is going to be a downer. So I'm hanging up. Bye."

Long after the line went dead, pain and frustration snaked through me.

CHAPTER 21

I dropped off my work at the bank, then we went out for breakfast. As I sat in the booth across from Summer, I couldn't help but compare the girl I'd picked up at the airport weeks ago, and the girl sitting here now.

Her sullen expression had vanished, replaced with a vibrancy that spoke of happiness and the hope for a bright future. She still used black eyeliner and mascara, but her flawless complexion went untouched. She wore minimal lipstick and her hair, like the Maine weather, changed frequently.

I enjoyed her smile and the twinkle in her eyes.

"Why are you staring at me?" Summer asked.

"I was thinking how much I'll miss you."

Looking embarrassed, she ducked her head. Fortunately the waitress arrived to take our orders so the awkward moment passed.

Several minutes later Summer dug into her stack of blueberry pancakes. "These are good, but not nearly as good as yours."

"You always say that when we come here. I don't understand why you don't order something else."

With an impish grin, she chuckled. "Because I can never get enough blueberry pancakes, that's why. And yes, it's what I want tomorrow morning for our last breakfast alone together. And again on Sunday for our breakfast with my mom." She squeezed her eyes shut for a moment. "I can't believe she's arriving tomorrow afternoon. I can't wait to show her how good I can read."

My heart thudded against my ribs. My life would seem empty after Summer left. "I'm sure she'll be impressed."

Again she chuckled. "My mom doesn't do impressed. She'll be *wowed!*"

A painful twinge reminded me of the last time Dana used that expression. I forced a laugh, lifted my cup and drank some of my lukewarm coffee.

Summer grabbed the menu. "See this," she said pointing to a dessert. "This says brownie. And here's ice cream. Beer," she added, nodding to the gold lettering on a small advertisement on the table.

The letters formed the word *Bud*—on the line below, Budweiser—but I didn't correct her. My teaching days were over, and I was determined to enjoy the little time we had left together.

After breakfast, we headed to Day's Jewelers to pick out a charm for her bracelet. Summer took considerable time looking at the display.

"Here's one of a basketball," I said, thinking it was perfect.

"Maybe I'll get that one next time I visit you."

My spirits lifted. I'd been walking around in a gloomy mood. She'd visit often. Instead of looking at today as our time together ending, I needed to think of the many times in the future Summer would spend in Maine. "I'm surprised you don't want the basketball."

"I'm looking for something even more special than a basketball."

"I didn't realize there was such a thing."

The saleslady leaned over the glass case. "Do you have something particular in mind?"

"Yes, a book."

"Here's one," the saleslady said, setting a small box in front of Summer with a miniature gold book.

"I want to have it engraved," she said, turning to me. "I'd like an A, for Annie, on the tiny cover to remind me of everything you've done for me."

In that instant, any residual gloom dissipated. Tears welled in my eyes.

Once I'd regained control, I turned to the saleslady and asked, "Can we have it engraved today?"

"I'll check with the jeweler." She returned a moment later to say we could pick up the charm in an hour.

I pointed to the basketball charm. "We'll take that one, too. That's if you want it?" I asked Summer.

"Cool!"

* * *

Later that night Summer helped me carry in wood from the garage. I hadn't used the fireplace since Paul died, and when Summer asked me if we could have a fire, I hesitated a moment. But I couldn't refuse.

Later while watching the flickering flames, I discovered that whatever demons I'd expected to haunt me never materialized.

"This is sooooo cool," Summer said, putting her purchases on the floor in front of the hearth.

We'd picked up chicken lo mein and eggs rolls, her favorites, to eat while we worked. Summer had insisted on buying supplies to make a welcome sign for Dana.

Kneeling in front of the coffee table, Summer ate a bite of lo mein, then pulled a bright yellow poster board from a bag. Holding a red marker, she spelled out, WELLCOME MOM in large crooked letters.

The spelling wasn't perfect but that wasn't important. She then sat next to me on the couch and ate an egg roll, dipping into the plastic container of duck sauce before each bite.

She lifted her arm and watched the swaying charms. "This is just the coolest bracelet."

"I'm glad you like it." I hated to ruin the mood, but I had to warn her so she'd be prepared. "Your mom's done well in rehab, but you need to be aware that she could fall back into her old habits."

"She won't. Mom says this time she has it licked. This time, she's going to be all right."

"I'm sure she will be, but just in case there's a problem, I want you to promise you'll call me right away."

Summer nodded and smiled. "Okay."

But I could tell she didn't think my warning was necessary. I hoped she was right. "Promise?"

"I promise."

After we finished our meal, Summer jumped to her feet. "Time to *wow* up our poster."

An hour later, glitter clinging to our hands and clothing, we leaned our handiwork against the couch and stood back.

"That looks great," I said, admiring our gaudy but extremely talented efforts.

"When Mom sees this, she's totally gonna freak."

Under a gray sky, snow drifted down lazily when we pulled into the parking garage at the Portland International Jetport. We'd stopped by a florist so that Summer could buy her mother a rose just like the one Randy had given her.

Summer was up early, and I hadn't slept all night. My right side twisted with another cramp, which I ignored. During the night, I hoped against hope that a miracle had happened and Dana had transformed herself into a decent mother. I doubted it, and the thought of what I might have to do—and how it would upset

Summer—nagged at me. I hoped my worries were needless.

I parked the car and opened the door. Summer jumped out, her poster in one hand, the red rose in the other. "Hurry, we don't wanna be late."

I laughed. "We're forty minutes early."

"The plane could be early."

I had to dash at a steady clip to keep up with Summer. Her poster swung by her side. The red on the W ran a little when the snow landed on our sign. Summer seemed oblivious to the problem. Soon we were inside the terminal checking out the flight schedule.

"Thank goodness, the plane is on time," Summer said, hopping from one foot to the other. "I don't think I could wait one minute longer." She giggled nervously and glanced at me for a moment.

My uneasiness intensified. "Do you have something on your mind?"

"Yeah, but it's kinda dorky."

I shook my head. "Dorky?"

"Yeah, I just want to say thanks for all you've done. I figured I should say it now because when my mom arrives, I'm gonna probably be very busy, and I don't want to forget to say it. Also, there's one more thing I gotta say."

She leaned in close and kissed my right cheek. "I love you, Annie. Thanks for putting up with me."

Caught off guard, I felt tears rimming my eyes.

"Thank-yous aren't necessary. I enjoyed having you here with me. And I'm going to miss you a bunch. I love you, too, Summer." *More than you'll ever know.*

Summer gave a wobbly smile and knelt to tie her combat boot, which gave me a chance to regroup.

Half an hour later we stood by the windows watching the planes land and take off. Dana's plane had landed, but we didn't know which one was hers. As we waited for her to walk through the glass revolving doors, Summer stood on a chair, craning her neck, trying to see farther. "Ohmygod, I think I see her. Yeah, that's her. She's coming."

My heart leaped.

Please, let everything be all right.

Long sigh. "No, it's not her."

We waited for several more minutes, but Dana didn't walk through the doors.

"Maybe she was the last one off the plane," Summer suggested.

"That's possible."

"Or maybe she's using the ladies' room."

I nodded. But I was losing hope rapidly.

Summer's face paled. Her fingers were wrapped so tightly around the stem that the rose sagged over her palm.

We went to the desk, and I asked the attendant to please check her computer. I handed her the paperwork about Dana's flight and her seat on the plane.

After reading the information I'd given her, she typed on her keyboard and watched the monitor. "That flight has definitely landed. And according to my records, all the passengers have disembarked."

"Could you check to see whether my mom was on that plane?" Summer asked, her eyes dull, listless, a hollow ring to her voice.

The attendant glanced at her monitor again. "It says here that passenger never showed up for her flight. They gave her seat to someone flying standby."

Summer swore.

People turned and stared.

Tears streaming down her face, she threw the rose at her feet and stomped on it, tore up the poster and shoved it into a nearby trash can.

My anger toward Dana flared. "Maybe your mother called after we left. I'm sure she has a good reason," I said to calm Summer.

"That's crap, and you know it."

CHAPTER 22

As I drove home, Summer kept her head turned from me. Her shoulders trembled as she sobbed.

"I know you're disappointed, but let's wait until we talk to your mom before getting too upset. Maybe her rehab program lasted a few days longer than expected."

"That's crap, and you know it."

Steering around a parked car, I focused on the road, which had begun to ice over. "We should give your mother a chance to defend herself."

"I guess."

Meanwhile, my fingers clenched the steering wheel. No excuse Dana came up with would satisfy me. No excuse would make up for the pain she'd caused Summer.

My right side cramped. I held my breath until the pain subsided and cursed Dana's insensitivity. First thing Monday morning, I'd check with an attorney to see what I needed to do to become Summer's permanent guardian.

When I pulled into the garage, Summer hurried inside, I assumed to check the phone for messages.

Prove me wrong, Dana. Please let there be a phone call

from you with an explanation. Any reasonable excuse will do. For Summer's sake, please don't let her down again.

But when I entered the living room, Summer was already on her way up the stairs.

"No messages?" I asked, which was evident. I'm sure if Dana had called, Summer would have told me.

"Mom's probably decided not to bother with me because I'm such a pain in the butt."

"We'll call Gram and see what she knows."

"I don't freaking care. I'm going to bed."

It was only six-thirty, much too early to go to sleep, but the disappointment of having Dana stand us up had wiped me out, too. "I'll come get you if she calls."

"Don't bother." The bedroom door slammed.

I called my mother and counted the rings—one, two. My stomach clenched, my side ached. Three, four.

"Hello."

"Mom, it's me, Annie. Dana hasn't shown up...."

"She didn't?"

"Summer and I just returned from the airport, and she never got on the plane."

"When I talked to Dana yesterday, she was excited about flying to Maine. She'd done so well in rehab this time, I'd hoped she'd follow through with her plans and build a good life for her and Summer."

"So had I. Do you suppose something went wrong, and that the doctors didn't discharge her?"

"Her program ended yesterday. She was planning to

spend the night with a friend and leave early this morning. I hope she's okay. I can't imagine her deliberately not getting on that plane."

Another sharp cramp.

I bent over and grabbed my side. "If you hear from her, call me right away."

"I sure will, and you do the same. Bye, Annie."

"Bye."

I hung up, my emotions tearing at me. When I remembered the disillusion on Summer's face, I hated my sister, hated her for what she'd done to my niece and the years of neglect. The next instant I imagined Dana run down by a car, and overwhelming guilt washed over me. Then I pictured her lying on the floor of some seedy motel room, overdosed, and drawing her last breath.

Hoping to ease my tension and lessen the cramping, I poured red wine into a goblet and took a few sips. Then I set the glass next to the phone, sat on the couch, and leaned my head back against the cushion.

I prayed for strength that I'd deal with this situation correctly. I prayed that Dana was all right. And more than anything, I prayed that Summer would not be permanently scarred by her mother's negligence.

Eventually, I dozed off.

Some time later, I was awakened by a ringing phone. Drowsy, I grabbed the receiver and dropped it at my feet. I scrambled to pick it up.

I heard Dana's voice. "Annie, I suppose you're about to flip out."

"Why weren't you on that plane?"

"At the last minute, I had a change of plans. I flew to Las Vegas instead."

"This has got to be the most selfish thing you've ever done."

She uttered a drunken giggle. "This is pretty much what I expected from you."

"You've been drinking."

"Only a couple glasses of champagne to celebrate."

"You just got out of rehab…."

"Look, I didn't call so you'd give me hell."

"Then why did you call?"

"To tell you my good news. I'm getting married."

"What about Summer?"

I heard a man's muted voice in the background.

More giggling. "I thought you wouldn't mind Summer visiting for a few more weeks until…after my honeymoon."

I pictured Dana and her man-of-the-moment making out, without any thought to her daughter.

For a moment, I wanted to hurt her the way she'd hurt Summer. I debated telling Dana I was going to file for custody, but I decided to wait until I was calmer, and Dana was sober. Besides, this was a conversation I preferred to have face-to-face—with a lawyer present.

I tried to ignore the pulsating pain in my side. "If you

think you can dump your daughter on my doorstep whenever you want, you're wrong. I'm through being used by you. And I'm through being Summer's temporary guardian whenever you decide to run off, or do drugs, or take a rehab vacation...."

A loud gasp interrupted me, and I jerked around to see Summer's face, the shock, the hurt, the disbelief.

"Honey, I didn't mean..."

She cleared the top step and shut the bedroom door so hard it bounced open before she slammed it again.

As I rushed upstairs, I debated whether to tell Summer that I planned to file for custody. Fearing it might add to her worries, I decided to postpone that talk until I'd had a chance to speak to a lawyer.

I tapped on the door.

"Get lost."

I pushed the door open and looked inside, saw her sitting against the headboard, staring straight ahead, Mr. T on her lap.

Earlier she'd reminded me of a small, wounded doe, defenseless and in pain. But now she looked lost. I rushed toward the bed, planning to hug her.

As I neared, her cold stare stopped me. "Summer..."

"Don't touch me."

"I want to explain..."

"Leave me alone."

"But you—"

"I don't wanna hear any crap right now."

Fearing I was making matters worse, I started to leave. As I reached the door, I turned. "Tomorrow we'll discuss your options. I know you're very disappointed, and you have good reason to be. I love you a lot. Remember that. You'll get to stay with me a bit longer. Is that so bad?"

She paused, ran her fingers through Mr. T's fur. When she looked at me, revulsion carved hard lines around her mouth. A shiver raced down my spine.

"I hate my mother."

"You don't mean that."

"Yes, I do. And I hate you, too."

CHAPTER 23

As I made my way down the stairs, I realized I needed to talk to someone. For a moment I considered calling Vi. But I quickly dismissed the idea. My limbs seemed heavy and awkward as I walked across the living room. Dana's call had knocked the breath from my lungs, the strength from my body. I was ready to collapse on the couch when I thought of the card with Randy's phone number. I needed help. He seemed like someone I could turn to. Was he home?

I went to the closet and dug the business card from my jacket pocket. My pulse pounding in my ears, I punched in his number. He answered on the third ring.

"Randy, this is Annie. I need you…" A sob squeezed past my throat.

"I'll be right there."

I wanted to tell him it wasn't necessary, that I shouldn't have called, that I was capable of handling this on my own. There was little he could do.

I tightened my grip on the phone.

"Please hurry."

I regretted calling Randy, despised the desperation in my voice. Since Paul's death, I'd taken pride in being strong, and even when I'd felt weak, I tried to appear confident. Since I couldn't take back the call, I hurried into the bathroom to wash my face. In the fluorescent lighting, as I glanced in the mirror, my complexion looked pale, the skin around my eyes sunken and lined with fatigue.

Dana was getting married to another drug addict.

She'd show up eventually, but not for a while. First she'd have her fun, and when she got bored, she'd come looking for Summer.

What would I do now?

I couldn't in good conscience let Dana take Summer back home, wherever that might be. Though I certainly looked forward to spending more time with my niece, I couldn't delay going back to work. Not if I wanted to keep my job. Yet Summer needed me now more than ever.

As another pain pinched my side, I winced. Slowly I breathed in, once, twice, three times, determined to ease the tension gripping me. Once my muscles relaxed, I gave myself a pep talk and brewed a pot of coffee. I looked forward to hearing Randy's opinion, but I was back in control.

I'd hire someone to tutor Summer. In another few months, she'd be reading well enough to reenter the school system. Until then, I'd ask Carrie if she could watch Summer on her days off. For the rest of the time, I'd pay a caretaker to come to my home. Where I'd find such a person was a mystery, but since I was determined to stay calm, I'd worry about that later. Maybe for a day or two Vi would agree to care for Summer.

When Randy knocked on the door I'd taken a carafe of coffee into the living room along with two cups and plates with slices of banana bread I'd made that morning.

He came inside and tossed his leather jacket over a chair. I sat on the couch and he sat next to me.

"What's up?" he asked, taking my hand, comforting me.

"Dana didn't show. She's in Las Vegas getting married to another rehab patient."

"How's Summer taking this?"

"Not well. She deserves so much more than what Dana's capable of giving her."

"I agree."

"I've been thinking of filing for custody, but I'm sure that entails a lot so I've decided to ask Dana to sign over custody of Summer."

"Will she do that?"

"I don't know. If she refuses, I'll check with a lawyer to find out what I need to do. It won't be easy, but I need to try."

"Summer's lucky to have an aunt like you willing to fight for her."

"Summer says she hates me," I said, battling tears and failing.

"And you believed her? That kid loves you. I'm sure of it." He reached for me and hugged me tight.

His touch filled the emptiness deep inside.

For a moment, I held him, drew comfort from having his arms around me.

His fingers brushed the back of my neck. "She needs time."

"I don't know what to do for her."

He pulled away, tucked a finger under my chin until I was looking up at him. "You aren't alone. I'll do everything I can to help."

His words reassured me, and at the same time left me wondering what I saw in his eyes. But now was not the time to find out.

He pulled away a little. "I'm going to call Greg and see whether he can come over here."

"You mean now? It's Saturday night."

"If he's free, he won't mind." Randy reached for the phone and punched in the numbers.

I hoped help was on the way. Although Greg couldn't perform miracles, Summer would benefit from speaking to a professional. And the sooner she opened up to him, the sooner she'd start to heal.

"Greg, call me when you get in," Randy said. "We

have a crisis. I'd like you to talk to Summer as soon as possible. Call my cell. Thanks."

Randy hung up. "His message says he's gone for the weekend."

I sighed, disappointment washing over me.

"Don't give up yet. Greg calls in for his messages so we might still hear back tonight. If not I'm sure he'll be in touch tomorrow morning."

"I want Summer to be happy."

"She's suffered a setback, but she's a strong kid. She'll be fine."

He reached for his cup. While he drank, I watched his Adam's apple bob up and down, admired his strong jaw.

"Thanks," I said.

"I haven't done anything."

"You came over here on snowy roads late at night. I'd say that's going above and beyond the call of duty."

"I'm not here because of a sense of duty. I'm here because I care."

I awoke the next morning stretched out on the couch, covered by a blanket, sunlight streaming through a slit in the drapes. It took a moment to figure out why I wasn't in bed and to remember last night's events.

As I sat up, I heard footsteps and saw Randy coming through the kitchen door.

"You've been here all night?" I asked.

"Did you know that you snore?"

"No way."

"Protest all you want, but I know better." He grinned. "Next time I'll get it on tape and prove it to you."

Next time?

My heart raced.

"If you'd like, I'll make breakfast while you get ready. I'm not much of a cook, but I do great toast, and I can hard-boil eggs to perfection," he said with a wink.

I stood. "I'll be right back. I want to check on Summer."

"She was asleep when I peeked in on her during the night and again an hour ago."

"Have you heard from Greg?"

"No, but I left another message."

After looking in on Summer and finding her asleep, I hurried into the bathroom to shower. I then went into the bedroom and pulled on jeans and a turtleneck. I ran a comb through my hair and decided to apply a little blush so I wouldn't look so pale. As I headed into the kitchen, I was filled with a sense of hope. My side hadn't cramped since Randy's arrival, reaffirming my suspicions that my pains were caused by tension.

Randy popped four slices of toast from the toaster. "I decided to use paper plates just in case I get stuck with the dishes. Better to err on the side of caution."

"I have a dishwasher."

"The dishes don't jump in there by themselves."

"Good point."

I sat down and ate slightly burnt toast with jam, along with a runny hard-boiled egg. I found myself comparing Randy's culinary skills to Tony's, whose skills rivaled the finest chefs. Tony's memory no longer caused the wrenching ache in my chest. I no longer missed his cooking—or him.

Randy buttered a piece of toast. "Did you tell Summer that you're going to ask her mother to allow her to stay with you?"

"I wanted to, but she wouldn't speak to me last night. I was afraid to make matters worse. If Summer stays with me, that would mean she won't be going back to see her friends."

"It might be better if she kept a distance from those kids."

"I know that, but I fear she'll look at staying in Maine as losing another part of herself."

We had a nice leisurely breakfast. I didn't remember toast tasting this good. I suspected it was due to the company.

He amused me with stories about work, and we chatted about everyday occurrences, the weather and my job at the bank. Figuring I should check on Summer again, I stood. What started as a dull ache, escalated. At first I ignored the discomfort, figured it would subside. What felt like a hot poker jabbed into me. I doubled over with pain, clutching my side, gasping for breath.

Randy jumped to his feet and picked me up. "What's wrong?"

"My side hurts a lot."

"I'm taking you to the emergency room." He set me down on the couch. "I'm going to wake up Summer and tell her to get dressed quickly."

The pain had already started to subside. "That's not necessary. I'm starting to feel better already."

"I saw how you looked. You should be seen by a doctor."

"I've been under a lot of stress lately. I'll make an appointment on Monday."

He stopped halfway up the stairs. "Stay still. I'm going to tell Summer to get dressed anyway, just in case we need to leave."

I heard him knocking on the door, calling out her name, then entering her bedroom. Randy cursed and ran down the stairs.

I jumped to my feet, ignoring the ache that came storming back again. "What's wrong?"

"Summer isn't in her room."

I rushed to see for myself. She'd taken most of her clothes and the box I'd purchased at the SPCA for Mr. T. "She's not coming back. She took the cat."

Three hours later Randy called. "Still no news, but every cop in the state is on the lookout for her. Are you having any more pain?"

"Don't worry about me. Just find Summer."

"I'd feel better if you called someone to come stay with you."

"I'll do that."

After he'd hung up, I realized I didn't want to be alone. I couldn't call Carrie because she and her boys were at Disney World. Mallory was at work, and though I knew she'd close her shop to be with me, I didn't want her to do that. So I phoned Vi.

"Hi, it's Annie."

"What's wrong, dear? You don't sound so good."

"Summer's run away again. The police are looking for her, and I don't want to be alone."

"I'll see you in a few minutes."

Vi arrived ten minutes later. "How long has she been gone?"

"I'm not sure, but she was in her room before breakfast."

"How did she get out without you seeing her?"

"I think she walked down the stairs and through the living room while I was in the kitchen...." Enjoying myself with Randy when I should have been focusing on Summer. "There are footsteps in the snow heading toward the street."

"Do the police know?"

"They're searching now."

"I'll make us a cup of tea." She cupped her hand over my elbow and steered me into the kitchen. "Sit down and rest, dear. You look like you've been dragged behind a car. Have you been sick?"

"I'm just tired." As she filled the kettle with water, I explained what had happened and why I thought Summer had run off.

"It's a crying shame what your sister has done to that child."

Later that afternoon, I convinced Vi I was fine by myself and that she should go shopping with her friend. Looking reluctant, she left, making me promise I'd call her the instant I heard any news.

Once she left, I paced across the living room. All day I'd had an intermittent ache in my side, but the pain was mild compared to this morning's attack. I was quite confident it was due to stress, but I'd still check with my doctor on Monday to be sure.

I spent the rest of the day sipping tea and nibbling crackers to ease my nausea that had started a few hours ago. When I passed a mirror, I was shocked to see my greenish pallor.

At six I watched the local news, fearing what I might hear or see. When the phone rang around ten, I rushed to answer it.

"Annie, I've found her," Randy said, sounding almost as relieved as I felt.

My knees gave way. I dropped onto the couch. "Is she all right?"

"She's fine. I should have her home in less than an hour."

CHAPTER 24

When Randy dropped off Summer, I ran to embrace her. "I'm relieved you're back…."

She pushed me away, stormed up the stairs and slammed the door.

"Where did you find her?" I asked.

"She was past the turnpike exit in Kittery trying to hitch a ride."

"She could have been…"

"Raped or killed," he said, his voice tough but filled with empathy. "I already pointed that out to her. She knows what she did was stupid."

"Where was she headed?"

"Back to L.A. to be with her friends."

My heart clenched. "She can't go back there by herself."

"I know, but it'll take time for her to accept that. I tried calling Greg again. As soon as I hear from him, I'll let you know."

"You're leaving?" So soon.

"As much as I'd like to stay, it's better for the two of

you to iron this out alone. And my shift doesn't end until seven tomorrow morning. But I'll drop over then to check up on you two."

I nodded. "Thanks…for everything."

His gaze lingered on me. I saw longing in his eyes. He inched closer, lowered his head a little. For a moment I thought he was going to kiss me.

The idea appealed.

A *lot*.

Instead his knuckles brushed the side of my face. "Take care of yourself."

"I'm fine."

"You don't look fine," he said. "I'm worried about you."

I was going to deny it, but knew he was right.

"If you need anything, call me no matter what time."

After he left, I marched up the stairs, steeling myself for a possible argument.

I knocked on the door. When Summer didn't respond, I let myself in.

Stone-faced, Summer stared straight ahead, patting Mr. T by her side.

I'd planned to sit on the bed beside her, but quickly changed my mind when I saw her cold expression, felt the anger pulsing from her rigid body.

"I was worried about you."

She didn't even blink.

"Taking off like that was a foolish thing to do." I had

no idea what to say. "You should have known better. You should have talked to me."

Dead silence.

"You're upset right now, but in time, some of the hurt you feel will go away. And the anger toward your mom will subside."

Ignoring me, she continued to run her fingers through the cat's fur.

"I'm trying really hard here. You need to talk to someone, and Greg isn't available so I'll have to do. I need you to assure me you aren't going to run off again tonight."

She glanced down and rubbed Mr. T's ears.

"Summer, talk to me, please."

Slowly, she lifted her head, her lower lip curling with disgust. "I want to get out of this hick state and go back where I belong…with my friends."

"You belong here with me."

"Yeah, right. I heard what you said. You don't want me any more than my mother does."

Disbelief flooded through me. "That's not true."

She laughed. "Yeah, right. I'd have to be really dumb to believe that."

"I'm going to ask your mother to let you stay here with me. I want to be your permanent guardian."

"That's a bunch of bull."

"It's the truth."

Her gaze traveled over my face as though she were

trying to decide whether to believe me. Then she sneered. "If it'll make you leave me alone, I promise not to take off tonight. So there, are you satisfied?" She inhaled a shaky breath and continued, "I don't need another mother."

"I know I can't take your mother's place, but I do want to provide you with a good, stable home, something your mother can't do right now. Surely, there's room in your life for an aunt who loves you very much."

She slid Mr. T off her lap and jumped up, her face inches from mine. "Let's get this straight. You aren't talking to a little kid. You accused my mother of dumping me on your doorstep. That sure doesn't sound like you wanted me."

"I was furious with your mom for what she'd done to you. I wanted to make it clear to her that she couldn't shuffle you back and forth every time she got herself in trouble. It's not fair to me or to you. I don't regret for a second that you're here, because I love you."

Some of the anger drained from her face. "You're just saying that."

"I've never lied to you. I want you here with me."

"That's crap." Some of the bluster had left her tone. Had part of what I'd said begun to sink in?

I knew she needed time to adjust to the idea. "Think about it. We'll talk more later when you've had a chance to decide how you feel about staying here with me."

She didn't reply, and I didn't expect her to.

I left the room, and quietly shut the door behind me. I went into my bedroom and took a pillow and blankets out onto the couch, planning to spend the night in the living room, hoping I'd wake up if Summer tried to leave.

As I dozed, I heard the clock chime every thirty minutes. Several times I went upstairs to make sure Summer was still there. Then I'd lie on the couch, pondering what to do next, vaguely aware of a dull ache in my side. I breathed slowly, deeply, determined to relax every muscle in my body. I tried to visualize my feet going limp, my knees, up into the abdomen, chest and arms.

Relax, take it easy.

Thinking a cup of tea might help, I stood, went into the kitchen, and poured water into a kettle. As the constant ache throbbed in my side, I focused on finding the tea bags. On the second shelf, I grabbed for the box in the cupboard. A gut-wrenching pain twisted inside, felt as though it were ripping me apart.

With an effort, I turned off the heat under the burner and staggered toward the living room, planning to lie down, hoping a new position would help. As I neared the couch, the pain knifed through me. I dropped to my knees, rolled onto the floor and balled up onto my side.

Something's very wrong.

I need help, and I need it now.

"Summer." I tried to shout, but my voice faded as my pain intensified. "Summer," I called out again, using the last of my strength.

Even if she heard me, she might not come.

Then I heard the pounding of footsteps. In a blur I saw her kneeling over me.

"Annie, what's wrong?"

"Hurt, my side."

"Should I call Vi?"

"No..." Vi and Summer together. Bad idea. But I had no choice. "Yes."

She ran to the phone. "Vi, Annie's sick. She's on the floor in a lot of pain, and I don't know what to do."

I clenched my teeth and tried not to scream as the muscles in my side spasmed.

"Yes, I will. Hurry," Summer said, hanging up and punching in numbers. "Please send an ambulance right away."

Don't. Not necessary. But I knew it was.

Summer gave the person on the phone our address. I heard the click of the front door being unlocked.

She rushed back to me, ran her fingers over my forehead. "Vi's on her way. She'll know what to do."

I made a feeble attempt to nod.

Through a pain-induced haze, I was aware of Vi's voice assuring me I was going to be all right as two attendants lifted me onto a gurney. In the background I could hear Summer crying. I wanted to comfort her, but they were already pushing me through the door. Though I didn't remember the ride to the hospital, I found myself in a room with bright overhead lights, and a kind-looking man peering down at me.

"Annie, I'm Doctor Paquette, where exactly do you hurt?"

"My right side."

"How long has this been going on?"

I shook my head. "A few days, a week. I'm not sure. I can't stay here. I need to go home." As I said the words, the doctor pressed on my side. I screamed.

"I'm ordering some blood tests and X-rays. But first the nurse will have you sign a few forms giving us permission to do surgery if necessary."

"What's wrong with me?"

"I can't be sure, but I think you might be having a gallbladder attack. You're jaundiced, and you exhibit the classic symptoms."

"How long will I have to stay in the hospital?"

"I'll know better after I've seen the test results." He walked away and made notes on a chart.

The nurse returned with a syringe. "I'm going to give you a shot for the pain so you might feel a bit woozy. Roll onto your side."

She helped me turn. I felt a pinch.

"Are you more comfortable on your side?" she asked.

"Yes."

She secured the strap over my waist and had an orderly push my stretcher down long corridors into the X-ray department. As I waited for my turn, I realized the shot had left me feeling light and giddy. I closed my eyes and enjoyed the freedom from the constant ache, enjoyed the feel of my body floating on air.

I felt a hand on mine. Even before I opened my eyes, I knew it was Randy.

Was his touch that familiar?

Impossible, yet I was certain it was him.

"What's wrong? No one here will tell me a damn thing," he asked.

"The doctor thinks it's my gallbladder."

"That's good news. My partner's wife had her gallbladder out last year. The operation was done in day surgery, and she was back at work in two days."

Just what I'd wanted to hear. "Good, because I can't stay here."

"Don't worry about Summer. Vi said to tell you the two of them will do fine."

"They don't get along. How will they spend a day or more together?"

"Let them worry about that. Your job is to get better." He leaned in close. "Will you promise me one thing?"

"Is that a trick question?" I asked. "I bet that medication the doctor gave me comes with a warning not to drive heavy machinery or make promises to sexy, rugged cops." I reached up and ran my index finger over his mustache.

So bold, so unlike me.

Ah, mystery solved.

His mustache was soft and tickled my finger.

He caught my hand in a steady grip and lowered his head until his lips brushed my cheek, the touch so light I questioned whether his mouth had made contact.

"I hope you aim better than that on the shooting range," I whispered, turning my face until he was only a breath away. I clamped a hand behind his head and pulled his mouth down, surprised by my bravado.

The kiss was gentle, insistent and too brief.

But definitely nice.

Nice and hot.

"That was much better," I said, licking my lips and sending him a saucy smile, which struck me as hilarious.

So I laughed.

His lower lip disappeared beneath his mustache when he grinned down at me. "You're buzzed."

"Yup," I replied, fluttering my lashes.

Then the pain in my side flared and cut through my haze. I bit down on my lower lip and cried out.

Randy's face mirrored my own fear.

The pain increased and didn't stop. The next hour went by in a blur: I cried, whimpered while I had

X-rays, had blood drawn, saw glimpses of Randy in the distance, worried, pacing.

I lay shivering on the cold X-ray table, covered with a thin sheet, my hands clenched, gritting my teeth.

A woman peered down at me. "I'm Doctor Wiseman. I've checked your tests. Your gallbladder is filled with tiny stones. One of the stones is blocking your bile duct, causing your pain."

I groaned. "Will I be able to go home tomorrow?"

"Usually gallbladder surgery doesn't require an overnight stay. But in your case, the incision will have to be a bit larger, which will require you to stay a few days."

"But…"

She pushed my hair off my forehead. "You don't have a choice. I don't want you to worry. This is routine surgery, and I've removed many gallbladders during my career."

Her soothing voice comforted me. Besides, as she'd pointed out, I had no choice. "Let's get this over with," I managed to say before a stronger pain struck, hard.

Someone pulled me onto a stretcher. Ceiling tiles overhead rushed by. I heard a clunk, felt a jolt as the wheels of the stretcher rolled into the elevator. Doors swung open and shut. More doors, hospital smells, I was moved onto a narrow table, squinted at the bright lights, people dressed in scrubs.

A man who introduced himself as the anesthesiologist examined my hand. "Your IV has infiltrated so I'll have to start another." He reached for something on a tray, then tapped his finger against my hand. "You're going to feel a small prick."

Small prick.

More bad news.

I giggled.

Then everything faded away.

CHAPTER 25

"Annie, can you hear me? Open your eyes."

I blinked an eye open and closed it again. Someone covered me with a warm blanket.

"You're in recovery. Let me know if you need anything."

I drifted back to sleep, woke up in bed in a room with large windows where I looked out at the stars in the sky and the lights to a Dunkin' Donuts across the street. A wide bandage covered a needle in my hand; an IV bag hung from a tall pole. I heard the slap of rubber soles and turned my head to see a nurse approaching.

"I need to take your vital signs."

She loosened the tie on my hospital gown and pressed an icy stethoscope against my chest. She was a pretty woman, in her early fifties; her long brown hair was pulled up in a bun. She listened for a few seconds, looped the stethoscope around her neck, then pressed two fingers against my wrist. Afterward, she pulled the sheet down and lifted my gown, checked my incision and murmured, "This looks good. If you have any discomfort, let me know. The doctor ordered meds for your pain."

"When can I go home?" I asked, feeling drowsy.

"Doctor Wiseman will be in later this morning. You'll have to ask her."

I drifted in and out of sleep, relieved to be pain free.

Someone brought in a breakfast tray, but I wasn't hungry. My stomach heaved at the thought of food.

A different nurse came in and took my vital signs, same routine, freezing stethoscope, cold hand on my wrist. She popped a thermometer in my mouth, took it out a minute later and jotted notes on my chart. "We have to get you up and walking."

With her help, I sat and stood on wobbly legs. Weak and light-headed, I managed to take a few steps and was exhausted when I finally got back in bed.

I fell asleep, dreamed about Dana and me playing with dolls, little kids, having fun, sometimes laughing, sometimes bickering. Summer was there, too, dressed in Goth, sneering at me from behind the door. Vi peeked into the bedroom window, waving her finger disapprovingly. What were they doing here? Confused I looked around, saw Edith waving folders, my assistant Roberta shaking her head. Mallory and Carrie joined the group and called my name.

"Annie, open your eyes. Can you hear me?"

Weighted down by incredible fatigue, I looked up, but just barely caught a glimpse of the doctor.

"You've developed pancreatitis," she said as the nurse pushed a thermometer into my mouth. I closed my eyes and took a much needed nap.

I heard parts of conversations and broken phrases— high temp, giving her antibiotics, the next twenty-four hours are critical—doors opening, phones ringing, foot-falls coming and going.

In a thick haze I heard Summer crying. "I'm sorry. I didn't mean it. I don't hate you. I said that to get back at you because I thought you wanted to get rid of me, too. You need to get well and come home. I miss you."

I felt warm all over, and happy, but incredibly tired.

"Shush," came Vi's soft voice. "Don't cry. Annie will get better."

"What if she doesn't?"

"She will. Because I said so."

Just like Vi, in charge, opinionated. A wonderful woman.

I almost smiled, but I couldn't find the energy.

Some time later, I was aware of someone kissing my cheek. A soft mustache tickling the side of my face.

Mmmmmmmmmm.

"Annie, I'm here, waiting for you to get better. A lot of people are praying that you recover soon." He sounded terrified.

Was I that sick?

Too tired to care, I drifted away again.

Feeling hungry, I awoke with the sun streaming

through the window. I glanced around and saw Randy asleep in the chair pulled against the bed. His clothes were wrinkled, his face in need of a shave.

"Randy," I whispered, my throat raw, my lips dry, thinking how handsome he looked.

He opened his eyes, grinned, jumped to his feet and took my hand, wove our fingers together. "You're awake."

"How long have I been sleeping?"

"You've been in and out of consciousness for four days."

"That long?" How could that be?

"You scared the hell out of me. You've been very sick, but you look great now. The antibiotics must have finally kicked in." He bent down and kissed me.

This time, right on target.

Edith came to visit. She brought cards from my co-workers and a bouquet of carnations. She handed me several envelopes, placed the vase of flowers on the windowsill, and turned to face me. "I don't want you to worry about your job. Take care of yourself and come back when you're up to it."

She slid her finger along the bedrail. "I called your house, and your mother-in-law told me your niece will be staying with you for a while."

"I hope she'll stay with me until she's ready to leave for college," I said, thinking I might lose my job.

"I expected as much…because you're dedicated, and I admire that in a woman. I've hired someone to fill in while you recuperate. That person will stay on and work part-time after you return. Which should cut down on the overtime you have to put in and allow you ample time to spend with your niece."

In that instant, a weight lifted from my shoulders.

Vi showed up the afternoon before I was due to go home. Until now, I'd avoided asking how she and Summer were getting along because the doctor had insisted I try to stay calm and stress free. Which wasn't possible when I thought of those two together.

When I saw the lines around her eyes, I knew she'd had a rough time. "You must be looking forward to getting back to your routine. I'm strong enough to take over tomorrow."

"Not on your life. Summer and I are going to pamper you after you get home," she said. "I've decided it's time to pass on my mother's ring, which is why I'm here tonight. I wanted to discuss it with you before I did anything."

I hadn't seen the ring since the day I'd told her about Tony. "What's up?"

She sat in the chair by the bed and ran her fingers over the small box she clutched in her hands. "I've learned a lot this last week. I've learned not to take anyone for granted because no one knows how long that

person could be around. You and I have had some issues lately. And I want to apologize for being such
a…bitch."

Her choice of words surprised me.

"Pardon the expression, but I couldn't think of anything else that fit."

"That's not so…"

"Now don't you go arguing with me. You know I'm
right. I had no business sticking my nose into your love
life. I've been an old fool, and I hope you can forgive me."

"There's nothing to forgive, and it turned out Tony
was a jerk."

"That may be so, but I had no right to lay a guilt trip
on you. You deserve to find someone who'll make you
happy. When you do, I only hope he treats you as well
as my Paul did."

I almost told her the truth, but when I saw the gleam
in her eyes as she thought of her son, I realized nothing would be gained by destroying her image of him.

Instead I smiled and looked as though I agreed.

But inside, I thought, *No way*.

I wanted so much more—a relationship with a man
who'd be faithful and love only me.

A one-woman man.

Like Randy.

Though it was too soon to know.

As I thought of him, my heart beat faster.

"I was an old fool about Summer, too. I should have

been more patient, instead of being judgmental and giving up on her. I wasn't being fair to her or to you. You needed my help, and I abandoned you."

"You did your best," I said, thinking of the hours she'd spent tutoring.

Vi handed me the box she'd been holding. "It's up to you what to do with this ring. I certainly don't want to hurt your feelings."

I opened the lid and admired a large emerald solitaire, the ring that had belonged to her mother.

Vi stood and covered my hand with hers. "This past week, Summer and I have grown very close. She's opened up to me and told me some things I found hard to believe. She's had a terrible life, and she feels as though she doesn't belong anywhere. I want to show her how much she means to me and this family. I couldn't love her more if she were my biological granddaughter."

Speechless, I sat on the side of the bed, trying to digest all she'd said.

"I don't blame you for looking shocked. So I've come here hoping you can help me decide. I want to give you my mother's ring. Rightfully, it should be yours, but I think Summer would benefit from it more. It may give her a sense of finally being part of a family."

Later that evening, Vi returned looking overly concerned.

"Is there something on your mind?"

"As a matter of fact, I'm worried about Summer. The last couple days she's seemed troubled. But when I ask her what's wrong, she says it's a matter she can only discuss with you. I hated to bring it up because I know you're supposed to be resting…"

"Where is Summer?"

"She's in the waiting room."

"Then send her in."

"Are you sure you're strong enough?"

"Of course. We're only going to talk, not go for a jog."

Vi left the room and a moment later, I heard a light knock. Summer entered, ducking her head as she walked across the room.

"Do you have something you want to tell me?" I asked, sitting on the edge of the bed.

She nodded and sat down on the chair, studied the pattern on the tile floor. "I've been thinking about what you said the other night about me living with you."

She clenched her fingers together, then pulled them apart. "I'd really like that, but I don't want to hurt my mom's feelings. And she might need me."

I realized their roles had been reversed for some time. "Your mother was fortunate to have you there to care for her."

"Vi told me that my mom got married so she might

not need me as much. But if that doesn't work out, she might need my help again."

It was a shame that Dana didn't feel this strongly about caring for Summer. Tears threatened. I did my best not to cry. In that instant I realized I couldn't ask Dana to give me custody of her daughter.

I wasn't sure she'd do that, but if she did, her signing that paper would sever the last fragile emotional tie between Summer and her mother.

What would that do to my niece?

"Summer, I don't want to come between you and your mother. If she stays off drugs, then in time, you can go back and live with her. But for a while, I'd like you to stay with me. Is that all right with you?"

She shuffled her boots under the chair. "I guess. I just don't want her to think I don't want to live with her."

"When I talk to her on the phone, I'll make that clear to her. All right?"

When she stood and wrapped her arms around my neck, I knew I'd made the right decision.

After Summer left, I couldn't stop thinking of our conversation. I decided the best way to deal with Dana was to appeal to her selfish nature.

I reached for my calling card and punched in the number Dana had given me. "Dana, it's Annie."

"If you're calling to give me a hard time, I'm going to hang up."

"No, nothing like that. I've been thinking about your good news the other night, and I have an idea."

"Yeah?"

"Since you're a newlywed, I thought I'd give you something special for your wedding."

"Like what?"

"How would you like me to take Summer off your hands for a while?"

"You mean it?"

"Sure." I crossed my fingers and waited.

"How long were you thinking of keeping her?"

"When I first got the idea, I thought maybe for a month or two, but that wouldn't be fair to Summer, because she'd have to switch schools midyear. So if it's okay with you, I thought I'd keep her here until June."

"Gee, I don't know…"

"A newly married couple needs time to get to know each other. I imagine that wouldn't be easy with a teenager around."

"Tell me about it," she said, laughing.

"Of course you can visit as often as you want. So do we have a deal?"

"It sure would be nice to have some free time."

As I waited, I started to count slowly to ten. One, two, three, four, five, six, seven…

"Sure, I'll do it."

"There is one thing I want you to do."

"I knew this was too good to be true."

"It's just a small favor. I'd like you to call Summer in a few days and tell her how much you're going to miss her. And I want you to call every week to talk to her so she knows you're thinking of her."

"All those long-distance calls can get pretty expensive."

"You can reverse the charges, or I'll send you a calling card."

"That would work," she said. "Is that it because when you called we were getting ready to go play slots?"

"Yes, I'm all set."

"Then bye. And thanks for taking care of Summer. It'll sure help get my marriage off to a good start."

She hung up, and I leaned against my pillow and relaxed. Although I'd have preferred a more permanent arrangement, I'd solved my immediate problem. Need be, I'd later seek legal advice, but first, I'd try diplomacy.

Randy drove me home the next day. I couldn't wait to be back in my own house again, sleep in my own bed, eat in my own kitchen.

He pulled into my driveway and hurried around to help me. I opened the door, swung my feet onto the snow-packed ground, and grabbed hold of his arm for support.

We'd stepped onto the stoop when Summer swung

open the door and took my hand. "Cool, you're finally home."

Hanging on the wall behind her was a large banner—Welcome Home, Annie—colored with markers and weighted down with glitter.

Vi rushed into the room. "Dear, if you need anything, anything at all, you just ask. We intend to make sure you don't overdo."

"I'm fine, honest."

Randy shut the door behind us, and I pulled free of everyone's hold to prove I could walk unassisted.

Vi took my coat, then hurried to move the coffee table a few inches away as though afraid I'd trip over it.

Summer guided Mr. T away from me when he stepped close to my legs.

Randy watched my every step and kept a hand extended ready to catch me should I fall.

Hoping to put their minds at ease, I sat on the couch and smiled.

Vi dashed into the kitchen, brought back a cup of tea, and set it down in front of me. "I put the kettle on when I first spotted you. I thought you might be thirsty. Are you ready for a nap?"

"No, I'm fine." In truth, the exertion of being checked out of the hospital and the short trip home had left me a bit tired. But I wasn't ready to go to bed yet.

Summer sat close to me on the couch, our legs touching, her hand stroking my arm.

Randy stood beside the couch as if on guard duty, ready to spring to action.

Summer leaned into me. "Look at my ring. It didn't fit so we put some tape around the band so I can still wear it until we can have it sized. It used to belong to Vi's mother. She wanted me to have it because she says I'm her granddaughter. I have two grandmothers now. Isn't that cool?"

I held her hand and admired the emerald on her finger.

"That's very cool," I said, smiling up at Vi, thankful she was wise enough to know what needed to be done with her mother's ring.

"Oh, I have a surprise for you," Summer said, jumping up and running up the stairs into her bedroom.

Randy used that opportunity to sit next to me.

I was tempted to kiss him, and I did, just a chaste peck on his check.

Vi busied herself with a napkin.

Randy winked and whispered in my ear. "We'll have to work on your aim later." He wrapped his arm over my shoulder and hugged me, made me feel special.

Summer returned a moment later with a notebook that had a photo of her and Mr. T on the cover. "While you were in the hospital, Vi helped me keep a diary for you to read when you got back home. Vi helped me form my letters much neater, and my spelling is getting really good."

"The girl's a genius," Vi said, proudly.

Summer glanced at the older woman, and they exchanged smiles.

Summer put the book in my hands.

I opened the cover and read the first two lines. "When I saw Annie on the floor, I was afraid she'd die. I was afraid I wouldn't get the chance to tell her that I love her...."

As I read each page, some heartfelt, some dealing with Mr. T's silly antics, or accounts of what Summer and Vi had done together in my absence, a wave of emotion flowed over me. I knew what it meant to love and be loved unconditionally.

Vi had her faults, but then, so did I. Summer would at times pout, cry and say things she didn't mean.

Yet I loved them, and they loved me.

Together, we could deal with the good and the bad times.

Because we were a family.

The colder the winter, the sweeter the blackberries will be once spring arrives.

Will the Kimball women discover the promise of a beautiful spring?

Blackberry WINTER

Cheryl REAVIS

A bear ate my ex, and that's okay.

Stacy Kavanaugh is convinced
that her ex's recent disappearance
in the mountains is the worst
thing that can happen to her.
In the next two weeks, she'll
discover how wrong she really is!

Grin and Bear It
Leslie LaFoy

REQUEST YOUR FREE BOOKS!

2 FREE NOVELS TO INTRODUCE YOU TO OUR BRAND-NEW LINE!

There's the life you planned. And there's what comes next.

Starting over was never easy, but something's gotta give!

In eleven short months, Charlotte Wagner-Smith has lost her husband and her job, driven over 1500 miles with two cranky kids and moved in with her mother-in-law.

Tanya Michaels

DATING
the Mrs. SMITHS

HARLEQUIN
Next™

HN18TALL

Available November 2005
TheNextNovel.com

They were a father and daughter who had never been close but something about rebuilding the lighthouse made sense.

Could a beacon of light that had always brought people home be able to bring understanding and peace to two grieving hearts?

the LIGHTHOUSE
MARY SCHRAMSKI

HARLEQUIN®
Next™

Holiday to-do list:

```
F Amo
Amos, Diane
A long walk home
```